PRAISE FOR THE MADISON NIGHT
MYSTERY SERIES

"A terrific mystery is always in fashion—and this one is sleek, chic and constantly surprising. Vallere's smart styling and wry humor combine for a fresh and original page-turner —it'll have you eagerly awaiting her next appealing adventure. I'm a fan!"

— Hank Phillippi Ryan,
Agatha, Anthony, Macavity and Mary Higgins Clark Award-Winning Author of *The Other Woman*

"All of us who fell in love with Madison Night in *Pillow Stalk* will be rooting for her when the past comes back to haunt her in *That Touch of Ink*. The suspense is intense, the plot is hot and the style is to die for. A thoroughly entertaining entry in this enjoyable series."

— Catriona McPherson,

Agatha Award-Winning Author of the Dandy Gilver Mystery Series

"A fast-paced mystery with fab fashions, an appealing heroine, and a clever twist, *That Touch of Ink* is especially for fans of all things mid-century modern."

— *ReadertoReader.com*

"Vallere has crafted an extremely unique mystery series with an intelligent heroine whose appeal will never go out of style."

– *Kings River Life Magazine*

"Diane Vallere...has a wonderful touch, bringing in the design elements and influences of the '50s and '60s era many of us hold dear while keeping a strong focus on what it means in modern times to be a woman in business for herself, starting over."

— *Fresh Fiction*

"A humorous yet adventurous read of mystery, very much worth considering."

— Paul Vogel,
Midwest Book Review

"Make room for Vallere's tremendously fun homage. Imbuing her story with plenty of mid-century modern decorating and fashion tips...Her disarmingly honest lead and two hunky sidekicks will appeal to all fashionistas and antiques types and have romance crossover appeal."

— *Library Journal*

"A multifaceted story...plenty of surprises...And what an ending!"

— Mary Marks,
New York Journal of Books

"If you are looking for an unconventional mystery with a snarky, no-nonsense main character, this is it...Instead of clashing, humor and danger meld perfectly, and there's a cliffhanger that will make your jaw drop."

— Abigail Ortlieb,
RT Book Reviews

"A charming modern tribute to Doris Day movies and the retro era of the '50s, including murders, escalating danger, romance...and a puppy!"

— Linda O. Johnston,
Author of the Pet Rescue Mysteries

"I love mysteries where I can't figure out who the real killer is until the end, and this was one of those. The novel was well written, moved at a smooth pace, and Madison's character was a riot."

— *ChickLit Plus*

"Strong mysteries, an excellent cast, chills, thrills and laughter, and an adorable dog... if you haven't read a Madison Night mystery, what are you waiting for?" — *Kittling Books*

"The writing was crisp with a solid plot that kept me engaged with Madison, Tex and the other supporting cast." — *Dru's Book Musing*

"The strength of this series that Madison has changed, adapted, and grown over the course of the six books." — *3 no 7 Looks at Books*

"...a well plotted mystery filled with great characters that will keep you hooked until you get to the final page." — *Carstairs Considers*

THE KILL OF IT ALL

A Madison Night Mystery

THE KILL OF IT ALL

Madison Night Mad for Mod Mystery #9

A Polyester Press Mystery

Polyester Press

www.polyesterpress.com

Cover design by Diane Vallere. Rocky (dog) Artwork © Henery Press, used with permission

eBook ISBN: 9781954579286

Paperback ISBN: 9781954579293

Hardcover ISBN: 9781954579392

THE KILL OF IT ALL

A Madison Night Mystery

Diane Vallere

Polyester Press

for Donald Vallere

ONE

THE PITCH MADE IT SOUND GLAMOROUS. A THIRTY-SECOND commercial aimed at new homeowners featuring a local decorator who reeked of genuine charm and a surprising dearth of experience. Filmed in her studio, surrounded with classic pieces of furniture that represented her flair with mid-century modern design. At least that was the concept. My concept. I was the local decorator in question.

My plan was to buy local TV spots and ad space at the local cinema house that ran classic movies. Who wouldn't pay attention to a perky blonde in colorful vintage when she was sandwiched between ads for plastic surgery and used cars?

The problem wasn't with the concept, it was in the execution. Decorating was my specialty, and being high on DIY, I naturally assumed I could do this myself too. I filmed a low-production commercial in my studio with my phone, edited it with free software from my computer, and added my contact information along the bottom. I sent it to the volunteer advertising manager for a local movie theater where I sometimes volunteered and hoped for the occasional spot.

But the volunteer advertising manager for the local movie theater was also the paid advertising manager for the local TV station, and when another advertiser backed out of his spot, mine was slotted in as the replacement. My phone exploded the next day: new clients, old friends, and more than one director who told me my charming, low-production concept would do my reputation more harm than good. From there, it was a hop, skip, and a jump to storyboards, cue cards, and a filming location in an airport hangar made to look like my studio. Acoustics or some such nonsense.

"Madison, I need you to relax." The instructions came from Denton Gold, the director of my commercial. Denton was in his late forties, had longish, thick gray hair and a soul patch of a beard directly below his lower lip. He wore round navy-blue glasses that framed his light blue eyes, a long-sleeved white mock turtleneck, and wrinkled khaki cargo pants that were cinched just above his hips with a belt from the military surplus store. "Your first few commercials introduced you as a local business owner. This time, we want you to talk to your audience as if you already know them. You want viewers to see you as a friend. You want them to want to hire you."

I sighed. A makeup woman came over to me and patted some powder onto my forehead. "This isn't the most relaxing setting," I replied.

"It's supposed to feel like your showroom," Denton said.

I glanced around. "It feels like an airport hangar."

I turned and looked at the enlarged backdrop behind me. A photographer had come to Mad for Mod and photographed a staged setting of furniture then had the image blown up and clamped onto a metal frame with Cardellini clamps. A staging crew attached beadboard to the bottom of a four-foot-square portable wall, and a gaffer aimed a 300D Mark II light at me. Production assistants bustled about and seemed to be everywhere and nowhere all at once.

"Let's go again," Denton instructed. "Talk to the camera like you're at a cocktail party."

I faced the camera and forced a smile. Denton pointed at me and nodded his head. One of the production assistants, the female, adjusted her grip on the cue cards.

"Hello, I'm Madison Night. I heard you recently bought a new house, and I'd love to help you customize it. I own Mad for Mod, a boutique decorating firm in Lakewood, and—" The spotlight temporarily blinded me, and instinctively, I shielded my eyes so I could see the words on the card.

"Cut," Denton called. The PA lowered the cards. "Madison, you have to read without looking like you're reading. If you shield your eyes from the lights, you're signaling to the audience that you're on a film set. Let's get this last take, and we'll call it a day."

Before I could properly express how much easier that would be if we were in my showroom like I'd originally suggested, a set of metal doors opened at the end of the hangar, and loud female laughter filled the space. Had the light not blinded me and ruined my take, it would still have been worthless. I turned to look and saw a curvy redhead in a bathrobe followed by several hunky police officers. None of them seemed to show the same curiosity about us.

Denton checked his watch and cursed. "They're early," he muttered to no one in particular. He walked away, leaving me and the rest of our commercial film crew unattended. That action had a ripple effect through the crew, who immediately acted like they were on a break.

"I'll talk to them," I said. I left my mock studio and walked to the new arrivals. As I approached, I forced a smile. It felt about as genuine as the one I'd used on set. Two of the buff policemen noticed me first, and one by one, the group quieted.

"Hello," I said. "We're filming a commercial over there. We're almost done. Would it be possible for you to keep it down while we finish, or maybe even wait outside?" I turned up the dial on my charm and tipped my head to the side. "If I can get my lines right, I'm sure we'll be finished in no time."

The redhead in the bathrobe smiled back at me, but her smile was more of the cat-and-the-canary version. "I'm sure you're done now," she said. She held my stare long enough to make me self-conscious, and considering I was fully clothed and she was not, it was a point scored in her column. As if to underscore the point, she untied the belt of her bathrobe and eased it back over her bare shoulders.

Her fingernails, long, pointed pink talons with tiny sparkly faceted stones embedded in them, sparkled under the overhead lights. Underneath the robe, she wore a strapless pink lace bodysuit practically molded to her body, the kind of undergarment you might find on a Barbie doll in the sixties. She swept her red hair to the side, where it draped over her shoulder. "These boys caught me in an infraction of the law, and I need to be punished." The men tittered. The woman winked at me even though I was certainly not in on the joke.

Before I could process what she meant, Denton approached. "Olivia, you're early." He pulled her in, kissing her on each cheek. "We were just wrapping up this morning's shoot. I'll send the lighting crew over to set up yours." He turned to me and paused for an awkward moment before continuing. "Have you two met?"

"No," I said.

"Olivia, this is Madison Night. Madison, this is Olivia Jean."

"Hello," I said to Olivia.

"Charmed, I'm sure," she said. The caliber of her voice had risen to a girlish timber. I glanced behind her at the uniformed police officers, but they appeared not to have noticed. She waved her hand over her shoulder. "These are my men."

Up close, it was clear the men weren't actual police officers. I had the uneasy feeling the airport hangar was about to become the backdrop for something more risqué than a decorating commercial, and I had the sudden urge to return to my set and cover it in protective plastic.

"As I said, we're just wrapping up," Denton repeated. "I'll send hair and makeup over when we finish."

Denton turned away. I lingered and smiled again, but Olivia had already forgotten I was there. I caught up with Denton halfway back toward where we'd been filming my commercial. "I didn't realize we were almost done," I said then added, "I guess I didn't do as poorly as I thought."

"Olivia's here to film a series of feel-good campaigns for the city. She's not exactly known for her attention span, so if she's here and ready to go, I'm going to get the cameras on her. I think I can patch something together for you from the takes we got today, but you might want to practice your lines just in case."

"In case what?"

"In case your film is crap and we have to reshoot, which I'd say is a fifty percent possibility."

"I was that bad?"

"Can't say I'd hire you, and I own a 1958 ranch on Forest."

We'd reached our shooting set. I looked over Denton's shoulder at Olivia, who relaxed in a comfortable red leather chair while a white man and a black woman fussed over her hair and makeup.

"Olivia's an actress?" I asked.

"She's the talent," he said. "Pain in the ass to work with, but when the cameras roll, she knows what to do."

"Could I stick around to watch her?" I asked. "I might learn something I can use."

"Olivia likes a closed set so she can get comfortable, but if you take your time packing up, you might get a glimpse of the magic."

"Fair enough."

A member of my film crew pushed a large light past me, and I hopped out of the way so as not to get my feet caught up in the cables. I couldn't complain about my time being cut short; Denton had not only told me about the second job, but he also offered me a discount if I was willing to work around it.

I watched the scene across the hangar. Olivia seemed at home amongst the cast and crew. She flipped through note cards and then handed the deck to Denton. While the lighting crew checked the levels and the set designer rolled in her backdrop on wheels, she went over her lines with the other actors. I was too far away to hear what they said, but even from a distance, I recognized the cooperation amongst the players.

I found myself entranced by how natural Olivia seemed even while barely dressed. If I could appropriate half of her confidence while reciting my lines, I'd have a genuine winning commercial on my hands. This was a learning moment, I realized. I knew how to expand my newly relaunched business, but until recently, the only advertising I'd done had been word of mouth.

As I stood behind the makeup chair, watching Olivia act, I felt another person behind me. "She makes it look easy, doesn't she?" Aliyah, the hairstylist, said. Her thick braids were knotted at the back of her head and hung down between her shoulder blades. Her skin was a rich brown, with expertly applied makeup that gave her an airbrushed appearance in the flesh. She had a hairbrush tucked under her arm, and she chipped away at the base of her fingernail while staring across the room. "You never know if experience like hers is going to translate into commercial work, but from what I've seen, she's a natural."

"I wish I could be like her," I said wistfully.

"No, you don't," she said. "She memorized lines that someone else wrote. You speak from your heart."

I laughed. "Yes, but I flubbed so much of what I wanted to say that a production assistant had to write it on cue cards."

She shook her head and gestured for me to sit down while she smoothed out my hair. "That was Denton's idea. Your early takes were better. Even when you tripped over your words, you were genuine. Olivia's paid to say what someone else tells her to say, and she's going to get attention because she looks like she looks. But it's not the direction I would go if I were the client."

"Who is the client?" I asked. "Denton said she was filming something for the city, but he didn't say who."

"Some not-for-profit," Aliyah said with a shrug.

I plastered on my fake smile one more time. "You mentioned Olivia's experience. What does she do when she's not filming commercials?"

"She's a dancer at Jumbos," she said. "It's quite the cop hangout, and from what I hear, she comes highly recommended."

TWO

I WOULDN'T ADMIT IT TO MOST PEOPLE, BUT I'D BEEN TO Jumbos, and not just the parking lot. I'd followed my policeman friend inside, and I knew firsthand that Aliyah was right. Jumbos was a booming business dominated by an off-duty cop clientele. I'd even gotten to know a former dancer who left the club to go freelance. She made enough money in six months to buy out the previous owner, turning Jumbos into a female-owned business and confusing feminists all over the state.

Aliyah tossed several compacts into a black nylon bag, zipped it shut, and grabbed another, bigger bag filled with lipsticks. She hoisted the bag onto her shoulder and leaned to the opposite side to offset the weight. "Good luck with your business," she said. "I hope your commercial brings you lots of leads."

I tore my attention from Olivia and directed it fully to

Aliyah. "I'll see you tomorrow morning when we resume, won't I?"

She shook her head. "Nope. I'm done here." She jutted her chin toward the film crew on the other side of the hangar. "Olivia—" She stopped speaking abruptly and shrugged. "Some jobs are a foot in the door to more opportunities, and some jobs are one-time gigs. Olivia is the talent, so what she says goes."

"She fired you?"

"She can't fire me, but it's not unusual for the talent to have their own hair-and-makeup team. We each have a four-hour minimum booking fee, so it's not cost effective for Denton to hire us both. You never know how these things are going to go." Aliyah readjusted the bag on her shoulder and gave me a tight-lipped smile. "Good luck, Madison."

"Good luck to you too." I watched the makeup artist walk away then resumed my task. I stretched the process of packing up my meager accessories out as long as I could while watching Olivia deliver her lines. After twenty minutes of spectating, I collected my cue cards and went home to practice in the mirror.

Home was a two-level house on a corner plot in the M streets of Lakewood, Texas. On the outskirts of Dallas, the Lakewood/White Rock Lake area was populated with a disproportionate number of mid-century homes and fans of the style. Flippers occasionally swooped in to buy up property, but the sterile monstrosities they left in the wake of their demolition stood out (and not in a good way) and rarely returned the profit the flippers desired. Being self-employed,

I'm as much a fan of entrepreneurialism as the next person, but I secretly enjoyed this flip on the flip.

The temperatures over the past few weeks had been gradually warming from the vestiges of Dallas winter, and today, it was in the mid-sixties. I'd packed several outfits for the commercial shoot so I could have options, and I'd finished in a yellow short-sleeved day frock with a jeweled collar, tone-on-tone buttons, and a cinched self-belt. It had previously been owned by Lisa Benton, a Mary Kay consultant in the early sixties. Her estate included a preponderance of pink and several black independent sales director suits, the oldest being a pristine wool two-piece ensemble with Texas-style cowboy hat from 1965, the year the suits were introduced. The suit was buried under layers of tissue along with a crate of never-used night cream, and though I'd never met Lisa, I imagined when she died, she looked young for her age.

I'd researched tips for dressing for on-air appearances and immediately ruled out anything red, white, or print. In addition to the yellow dress I wore home, I had an ivory suit trimmed in fox fur, a sleeveless green sheath with a metal daisy pin, and a pink mock-turtleneck top with matching trousers. My closet was the result of years of buying out estates. I'd accumulated it through a series of timely bids on estates I identified by reading the obituaries. Unsure as I was about how prospective clients might feel about my business strategy, I left the details out of the commercial.

Despite being responsible for the annual taxes on my property, I still thought of my house as belonging to the original owner, Thelma Johnson. Her husband had died shortly after they purchased the place, and she'd kept it, raised two kids, and eventually passed away when she was in her late seventies. A series of events had led to me obtaining it for the low price of the back taxes a few years ago. Even though the house now belonged to me, I couldn't bring myself to think of it as anything but hers. She'd become a part of my life, one of the many strong women who I'd discovered through the journey of building Mad for Mod.

I parked in the detached garage and approached the house. The storm cellar doors were open, and sounds of activity came from down below. There was one person who had access to my storm cellar aside from me, but that didn't make me any less cautious. When I was two feet away, a fluffy caramel Shih Tzu appeared and bounded toward me, followed by a Shi Chi with matching coloration. The dogs yipped their hellos. Moments later, their appearance was followed by that of former toxic bachelor Tex Allen, captain of the Lakewood Police department and current leading man in the movie of my life.

"You're back earlier than I expected," I said.

In the past two months, Tex had attended six different college fairs to recruit for the upcoming police academy. Citywide budget cuts and improved hiring packages at local businesses had made it difficult to woo potential candidates, but Tex was determined to fill his open positions with a new breed of cop. Since becoming the captain, he had changed the appearance of his precinct from mostly white males to robustly diverse, including two of the best interrogators in the state. The man loved a challenge.

Speaking of new appearances, today, Tex wore a frilly

white apron printed with drawings of kitchen appliances tied over a white polo shirt and medium-blue jeans, and he smelled...not fresh. As I got closer, he leaned in for a kiss, and I held up both hands to halt him.

"What's that?" I asked, pointing to the apron.

"Fish guts."

I raised my eyebrows. "I meant the apron."

"Borrowed it. You don't mind, right? I'll give it back when we're done."

"Keep it," I said. "I doubt there's a detergent strong enough to eradicate that scent, and I'm enjoying the vision of you in an apron. In fact," I added, "there's more in the attic. Perhaps you'd like an assortment?"

Tex grinned. There was something disarming about his smile that still hit me the way it did the first time we met. He'd matured a lot since that first meeting, and for all my tumultuous life changes, it was nice to have him as my constant. Plus, I'd gotten past the urge to slap him, which illustrated my willingness to evolve too.

While I stood with the dogs hopping around my legs, Tex went to the outdoor water valve and rinsed his hands. He dried them on the dirty apron then untied the apron and hosed it down too. After he turned the water off, he was damp from the spray of water, but he smelled considerably better. The Shi Chi, Wojo, circled Tex's legs twice and then stood with paws on his knees and yipped. Tex scooped the dog up and stroked the fur on his head.

"I got back two hours ago. I'd love to hear how your commercial shoot went, but we're cutting it close. I need a shower. Care to join me?" He wiggled his eyebrows.

"Cutting it close for what?" Rocky, my Shih Tzu, pawed my knees to get picked up too. I bent down and ruffled the fur on his head. "Did you make dinner reservations?"

"I left a message with your director. Didn't you get it?"

"No. I never even saw Denton on his phone. Whatever it is, can we cancel? I had no idea how self-conscious a director could make me feel, and it would be nice to spend the night with a more appreciative audience."

He grinned again, this time at my expense. I tried to hide my embarrassment. "I'd love to see your outtakes," he said.

"I don't think there were any *in*takes. I couldn't loosen up. I had a hot flash while we were filming thanks to those big lights. They finally wrote a script on cue cards, but the first two versions were unreadable. I should have bought a billboard instead."

Tex draped his free arm around my shoulder and guided me to the door. Rocky trotted along by my feet and hopped up the concrete stairs ahead of us. I pulled open the screen door and let him into the solarium, and then Tex and I followed through the second door that opened onto my kitchen. I'd renovated it for my fiftieth birthday and found it was impossible to feel depressed when in here. The whole room was yellow: vinyl tile floor, tiled counters, and even the appliances. It was like standing on the disk floret at the center of a daisy.

Tex set Wojo on the floor, and he joined Rocky by the water bowls under the window. I set my garment bags and purse on the kitchen table and collapsed into a chair. "All I want to do is take a hot bath, put on my pajamas, and read in bed."

"Sorry, Night. Tonight isn't optional. I wish it were, but I have professional obligations too."

"You're a cop."

"Captain of the cops."

"Right. You're the boss. Just give yourself the night off."

"It's higher up than that. The police commissioner is throwing a dinner party, and he wants us there." He bent down and grabbed my hands to pull me to my feet. I leaned back so he wouldn't be successful.

"How long have you known about this?"

He glanced at the clock. "Four hours?" He dropped my hands. "It's the reason I'm home early. Listen, I know it was a last-minute invitation. There's a good chance someone else canceled and we were invited to fill seats. But my job is tenuous right now, and getting to spend time with the commissioner in an off-duty setting is an opportunity to bend his ear about the concerns facing my department."

"And me?" I asked weakly.

"The commissioner's wife specifically asked me to bring that lovely decorator I've been dating. Who knows? There might be some ear-bending opportunities for you too."

I extended my arms, and Tex pulled me to my feet. Looked like the day wasn't over yet.

THREE

A LITTLE OVER AN HOUR LATER, WE ARRIVED AT THE HOUSE OF
Commissioner Edward Fraleigh. I was delighted to discover
the Fraleighs lived in a late-Fifties ranch in Dixon Branch, a
small neighborhood northeast of White Rock Lake. Despite
Tex's invitation to shower together, I recognized our time-
saving need would be better served if we had fewer distrac-
tions. Thanks to the lingering scent of fish, for the first time
ever, his shower lasted longer than mine.

Despite my exhaustion, the shower and change of
clothes had perked me up. I dressed in a silver sheath with a
gold duster originally owned by Gloria Jean Minnick, a
hostess for Braniff Airways in 1963. I'd purchased her estate
in full when she passed away ten years ago and found her
wardrobe a mix of flight attendant uniforms and cocktail
wear. It made me curious about how much truth was
included in the tell-all book *Coffee, Tea or Me?*, which I found
stashed at the bottom of her makeup bag.

Tex wore a black suit, white shirt, and narrow tie. His hair was still damp. The job of captain for the Lakewood Police Department had come with a shift in wardrobe needs, and he'd eventually gotten comfortable in a suit. I knew he preferred jeans and a polo shirt, but these days, that was less obvious to the rest of the world.

He rang the bell, and the door was answered by a man in his sixties who bore a strong resemblance to one of the grandfathers from *Sixteen Candles*. He was about fifty pounds heavier than his frame required and carried the weight in his torso. He wore square black glasses with lenses that magnified his eyes, giving him an air of surprise.

"Captain Allen! Good of you to make it on such short notice." He held his hand out to Tex and they shook. "And you must be Madison. My wife's eager to meet you." He leaned in. "I think she wants to get your opinion on the decorating."

"I can already tell it's a lovely home," I said. "So many of the original mid-century houses in the area have been gutted and rebuilt. You're lucky to have found one with the original bones."

He straightened up. "Ask my wife about that," he said. "She'll go on for hours about how we ended up in this place if you let her."

Edward held the door open, and we entered. Inside, I spotted several men in suits not dissimilar to Tex's. I gave my duster to Edward, who whisked it away down some hallway, and I reached out for Tex's hand. He squeezed back. We'd kept our relationship quiet for so long that the idea of being a couple in public still triggered butterflies.

We entered the living room. I took two glasses of champagne from a tray and handed one to Tex. He took a sip and wrinkled his nose.

"Once a beer man, always a beer man?" I asked.

He raised the glass toward me. "At least you know I'll be okay to drive."

Before I had a chance to sell him on the considerable benefits of champagne of this caliber, an elegant brunette in a deep-green silk dress swept across the room toward us. "Captain Allen!" she proclaimed. "I'm so glad you could make it." She hugged him and then turned to me. "And Madison. The articles are right. You *do* look just like Doris Day."

She hugged me too. I wasn't expecting the display of affection, and a little champagne sloshed out of my flute and onto the back of her dress. Tex turned away and stifled a laugh.

"I'm Arlene Fraleigh, Edward's wife. Welcome to our home. I know this party is for the men, but I told Edward I wouldn't throw a party if I couldn't invite someone to talk to." She grabbed my hand and squeezed. "I hope I didn't tear you away from anything important."

"Just a hot bath and a good book," I said. It was impossible not to respond to the woman's friendly demeanor.

Arlene tucked her hand in the crook of my arm and steered me away from Tex. I glanced back over my shoulder. A circle of men had closed in around him, and he caught my eyes and shrugged.

For as awkward as I'd felt earlier while on camera, I felt myself relax tonight. The Fraleigh house had been decorated with taste and money. "Arlene, your husband hinted that there was a story behind your house," I said. "I'd love to hear it."

She led me to a vacant love seat, and we sat side by side. "Edward was born in this house," she said. "When his parents passed away five years ago, he inherited it. The offers to buy it poured in, but when he brought me out to see it, I fell in love a second time. We'd been married for twenty years at that point. The boys were grown and off in college, and we didn't need a lot of space, so I convinced him to keep it. We had the electric and plumbing updated, and here we are."

"The place is decorated immaculately. It suits the house."

"All but the powder room," she said wistfully. "It's not dreadful enough to redo completely, but there's something about wood paneling in a powder room that feels claustrophobic. Don't you agree?"

"I don't know. I'd have to see it before forming an opinion."

"Of course. Let's go!" She stood and pulled me to my feet. I hadn't been angling for an invitation, but before I knew it, she led me through a hallway and pulled me into a knotty pine half bath.

She was right. There was nothing wrong with the room, yet it felt small. I ran my hand over the glowing pine paneling. "I see your dilemma. It's original, and it's in pristine condition, but..."

"But it's the most depressing room in the house. I believe the reason it's in such good condition is because his mother agreed with me, and they never used it."

As Arlene led me out of the powder room and back to the party, she paused by each room and pointed out details that I appreciated. It wasn't just the wall and curtain treatments that captured my interest but the furniture as well. I complimented her on her selections, and she refused credit.

"Most of the furniture is original to the place. Edward's family owned a furniture wholesale store in Dallas." She leaned in and dropped her voice. "Edward inherited that too, and we had our pick of the inventory."

"Did you liquidate the rest?" I asked.

She smiled broadly. "There was never a suitable time. I used to check on the store occasionally, but eventually, I stopped going. It's been over a decade since I was there. I don't know how to value the inventory or who to call to get the best offer."

I didn't wait for an invitation. "I'd love to see it," I said. "I could advise you or perhaps even help you find a buyer." It took all the willpower I had to keep from making an offer sight unseen. "If you're available, I could come tomorrow after I finish filming."

"Filming? I thought you were a decorator. What are you filming?"

I explained to Arlene how part of my expansion strategy was to identify the right clients, and that included a commercial campaign. Her expression changed as I talked, but I couldn't tell which part of my reply bothered her. "If I remember my lines, I should finish the reshoot shortly after lunch. My afternoon is free."

"I see," she said. "Would you excuse me? I need to talk to my husband."

"Of course." She left me in the living room. I finished my champagne and set the empty flute on a tray in the corner then returned to the main room in search of Tex. He was speaking with a small group of men. They laughed in a way that suggested someone had told an inappropriate joke. For not the first and not the last time in my life, I was thankful my job didn't require me to humor anyone other than myself.

Arlene and Edward came out of the kitchen together. Edward interrupted the group. "Excuse me, gentlemen. My wife just had a suggestion that I think you'll all enjoy. Follow me into the den." He turned away and led the group down a hallway to a room outfitted with three sofas in a U-formation and a large-screen TV. A square wooden coffee table sat in the middle of the sofas, and a Hazel Atlas Spaghetti String Drizzle carousel snack tray sat in the middle filled with pistachios, peanuts, and ginger chips. I occasionally came across Hazel Atlas pieces in my estate purchases. This one was milk glass with gold drizzle, and the compartments of the carousel fit together in a brass base. It coordinated nicely with other brass accents in the room: the atomic starburst clock, the base of the floor lamp, and the abstract brass art mounted on the wall behind us.

What didn't fit in the room was the television. It was a seventy-inch screen that made it impossible to appreciate the decorating nuances. Regardless of the potential of this room, it had one purpose.

"Take a seat, everyone. There's plenty of room for all of you," Edward said. "I have a surprise. As you know, we've been looking at ways to change the perception of the Lakewood Police Department, and our image consultant thought a series of targeted commercials should be part of that blitz. I'm excited to say that I received a rough cut of today's commercial, and you're all going to get to see it first."

At the word "commercial," I felt myself squirm. I couldn't get away from it if I wanted to! Tex squeezed my hand, and I squeezed back.

Edward turned the TV on and dimmed the lights in the room. And suddenly, the screen filled with the image of Olivia Jean, the stripper-turned-spokesperson from the airplane hangar. She wore the strapless pink lace bodysuit I'd seen earlier and held her hands behind her back.

"Hello, I'm Olivia, and I've been a bad girl. It's a good thing there are so many policemen around to keep me in line." She turned slowly, revealing that she was in handcuffs. Her eyes never left the camera, though a glance around the room told me the men weren't looking at her face. She winked at the camera. A quick cut took us to a different scene in which Olivia wore a tight pink skirt suit. She was surrounded by men in tight police officer uniforms who looked like extras from *Magic Mike.*

"I'm an independent woman, but sometimes, I like to know I've got backup." She put her hands out to clear the way and separated from the group. The officers fell in line and followed. A third cut brought us to Olivia in a large jacuzzi. The wardrobe department had an easy time on this shot, as she appeared to be naked in a frothy pink bubble bath.

"At the end of the day, I relax, knowing my local police department is a phone call away." She reached an arm out of the water and tapped the screen of her cell phone and then closed her eyes and leaned back.

There was no way that commercial was going to do a bit of good for the Lakewood Police Department, and I certainly hoped I wasn't the only person in the room to see that. Tex's body was rigid next to me. I glanced at his face. His jawline was tight, and his eyes were narrowed. He'd implemented sensitivity training in his orientation, had changed the face of the department by casting a wider net when recruiting, and had made it a top priority for the police in his department to get to know the residents of Lakewood to help break down the walls between them. This commercial was a joke.

The commercial ended, and the screen filled with a test pattern of colorful bars. Edward stood and turned on the lights. The TV flickered, and then a different image filled the screen: mine. There was no sound to accompany me, but I remembered it clearly enough: awkwardly reading from cue cards because I was unable to speak coherently about my business while a camera was pointed in my direction. And then my mouth stopped moving, and I looked directly at the camera, hands on my hips, and shielded my eyes.

This was one of my commercial takes from earlier today. It was one thing to have told Tex about how I'd done but another to have him—and a room filled with his colleagues —see it firsthand.

The room was silent. Edward flicked on the lights. "Well, well. It turns out this wasn't the only surprise we had tonight. Madison, you didn't tell us you were an actress."

"I'd hardly use that word," I said politely.

"Nonsense," Arlene said. She watched me closely. "Madison, you have a natural charm about you, and I'm sure I'm not the only person here who wishes we had the sound to go with that image. I have an idea. Darling?" She looked up at her husband. "Why don't we have Madison do the commercial for the police?"

"Oh, no, I couldn't," I said quickly. "I don't even know if my director got any usable footage from today's shoot. Olivia was—" I scanned the faces around the room and searched for my next word.

"Olivia was a poor choice for the job," Arlene finished. "You know it and I know it and Captain Allen knows it. I'm certain every person in this room knows it. Isn't that right?" Arlene reached over the back of the sofa and put her hand on top of her husband's, but the gesture lacked the loving touch I expected. Edward had one possible response, which was unfortunate for me.

"Of course, dear. Olivia's out and Madison's in." He turned to me. "You don't mind, do you?"

FOUR

I PROTESTED. I DEMURRED. I INVOKED THE NEEDS OF MY business and my schedule and the conflict of interest because of Tex and threw in the kitchen sink for good measure. And yet by the time we left the party, I was on the hook as the new face of the Lakewood Police Department.

I handed Tex the keys to my Alfa Romeo and waited until we were both buckled up in our seats before speaking. "Did you hear that? Arlene was like a steamroller."

"I'll talk to Edward tomorrow, and we'll get someone else. Maybe Olivia can wear something a little less—a little more—you know."

I crossed my arms. In all the fuss about my dilemma, I'd forgotten all about Olivia. "You know her, don't you? She works at Jumbos."

"How do you know that?"

"The hairstylist on my set told me. She said Olivia was

there to film a public service announcement for the city. You could have told me."

"I didn't know." He kept his eyes on the road. Normally, when the two of us went out, we rode in Tex's Jeep, but there was something about cocktail attire that didn't quite go with off-road capabilities. Tex navigated the quiet streets of the Fraleighs' development and then reached the main road.

"I got the feeling Arlene's suggestion that I do it had more to do with getting Olivia off the project."

"That's possible," Tex said. "Olivia *worked* at Jumbos. Past tense. A lot of the dancers left after the new ownership came on board, but that's not entirely unexpected. Jumbos is more of a stepping-stone than a long-term career choice."

I considered asking him how he knew, but it seemed the sort of question that was better left unasked.

THE NEXT MORNING, I woke early and went to the pool to get in my morning laps.

Tex had stayed over and took the dogs, so I'd be unencumbered for the day. I was fueled by the potential for humiliation in my near future and the desire to work out any stresses so I could appear relaxed when the cameras rolled. I barely paused between laps to chat with the seniors who populated the rest of the pool at this hour, eventually finishing and heading to the locker room for a shower and change.

I dressed in the pink turtleneck and matching trousers

from my commercial shoot, styled my wet hair with my
fingers, brightened my pale face with a perky pink lipstick,
and left. When I came out of the locker room, a man was
waiting for me.

"Madison Night?" he asked.

"Yes," I said. There was no point acting cagey; everyone
here knew my name, and chances were they'd already told
him where to find me.

He held out his card. "I'm Drew Billings. I work for
Edward Fraleigh. I have the details about your commercial."

"About that," I said. "I appreciate the offer, but I'm going
to pass. I'm sure if you tell Denton what you want, he can
direct Olivia into a more suitable performance."

"Olivia is out." He pulled an envelope out of his jacket
pocket and held it out. "This is a waiver. We all agreed
having you speak from the heart would be better than asking
you to memorize a script. You'll have more credibility if
you're not on the payroll, but we've arranged to pay you a flat
fee to cover your transportation costs."

"That's not necessary."

"Is ten thousand enough?"

We'd been walking side by side toward my car, but this
last statement stopped me in my tracks. "Ten thousand
dollars?"

"Yes, but between you and me, I can go to fifteen."

"Mr. Billings, I'm not sure I'm making myself clear. I'm
not an actor. I'm in a relationship with the captain of the
Lakewood PD, and I'm in the process of relaunching my
decorating business. Between the conflict of interest and my

lack of talent, I have neither the inclination nor the time to take this job."

"Twenty thousand," he countered. "Cash." He reached inside his other jacket pocket and pulled out another envelope. He handed it to me. "Directions to the set are inside. Mrs. Fraleigh thought you'd enjoy filming in a corner of her father-in-law's abandoned furniture store. They've arranged for hair, makeup, wardrobe. The crew was instructed to film a commercial for your business after you wrap with ours." He pressed his lips together and then continued. "I'd take advantage of that if I were you." Before I could form a protest, he tipped his hat at me and walked away, leaving me with a handful of cash, an offer to spend my day around new old-stock furniture, and an all-expense-paid opportunity to film a new commercial.

It wasn't a fair fight.

I waited until he drove away to peek inside the envelopes. Neat stacks of crisp hundred-dollar bills filled each, accompanied by a small white business card with an address printed on the back.

I drove home, grabbed my garment bags and train case, hopped back in the car, and drove south. Fraleigh Furniture was northwest of Fair Park, and it took me about fifteen minutes door to door. I parked in the lot next to a dirty brown Fiat and carried my belongings to the entrance. It was open, but no one was there to check me in.

Whatever resistance I'd had over this opportunity vanished the moment I went inside. Rows upon rows of chairs, sofas, tables, and bed frames from the fifties and sixties lined the floor. Piles of plastic and tarps had been tossed to the far side of the interior. I dumped my bags on the sales counter and went to examine the chairs.

Teak wood armchairs with floral cushions sat in a row. I lifted the cushion and saw Fagas straps—the dense upholsterer's webbing made of rubber inlaid with cloth mesh—woven neatly in near-perfect condition. I set the floral cushion back onto the chair and then lowered myself onto it. I got the same thrill sitting here as I did in any piece of mid-century furniture. Not only was it a piece of history that had survived generations and sell-offs, but, at least to me, it was beautiful.

I had lost myself in daydreams about what it must have been like for consumers to arrive at Fraleigh Furniture to decorate their new tract homes when I heard a noise from the back of the store. I turned in my chair and saw a thin brunette in an oversized white T-shirt and torn jeans creating a seating area. She had messy hair cut into a bob with bangs and wore round mirrored sunglasses even though it wasn't bright inside. A long silver pendant hung around her neck, resting a few inches above the brushed-silver buckle of a man's belt.

"Excuse me," I called out. The woman didn't respond. I called out again. She propped her knee on the cushion of the chair. She shielded her eyes and looked my direction. I waved. "I'm Madison Night. I'm supposed to film a commercial here. Are you part of the crew?"

I left my garment bags where they were and walked alongside the rows of chairs with the sunlight to my back. The deeper I went into the store, the more difficult it was to see. If we were going to film at the back, we'd need an expert lighting crew.

The young woman pushed her glasses on top of her head, revealing almond-shaped eyes framed with thick lashes. Aside from matte red lip color, she appeared not to wear makeup. Despite the vast differences in our age and our attire, I liked her immediately. I'd bonded with women over lipstick in the past and had found it to be a decent predictor of character.

"You're Madison?" she asked.

"Yes."

She held out her hand. "I'm Jules Staton."

I shook her hand. I felt something from her: curiosity? Judgment? An assessment of how well I may or may not appear on film?

"I'm the director," she added.

"Then you're the one I need to impress," I said lightly. I smiled.

Her eyes narrowed slightly, and her head cocked to the side. "He was right," she said. "You're the spitting image of Doris Day."

"Did you talk to Denton?" I asked, hoping their exchange was limited to my appearance and not my performance.

"I don't know a Denton," she said. She looked away and then down and then back at my face as if she were embarrassed. "I was the AD on the movie about that case you were involved in, the pillow stalkings?"

"The assistant director," I said slowly. The warm, fuzzy lipstick feelings I'd had toward Jules turned to an internal buzz, like the blood in my circulatory system had been replaced with club soda.

Several years ago, I'd helped solve a cold case that connected to a string of more recent murders. It was the case that introduced me to Tex, but it also involved my handyman-turned-ex-boyfriend, Hudson James. He'd been a suspect and was convicted in the court of public opinion long before I entered his life, and the result of the case led to a brief romance that left us both moving on in new directions.

A team of Hollywood producers had contacted Hudson about buying the rights to his story, and he'd made the deal. Occasionally, news about the movie's progress reached me, but I tried to avoid it where possible. The name Jules Staton shouldn't have meant anything to me except for one thing: Hudson had recently told me that he was engaged to her.

It was unclear if Jules knew of my personal connection to her fiancé or if this was simply a case of awkward coincidences. I was nervous enough about my performance. I didn't need to add that to the mix.

"I don't know much about the movie." I heard myself default to my Doris Day voice. "There's something odd about knowing your life is about to be splashed on a screen and there's not much you can do about it." I'd hoped to set her at ease, but she didn't have a reaction either way. I remembered this was the person responsible for filming me. "I'll do my best today, I promise."

Jules seemed preoccupied with something other than our introduction. She looked around and then put her hands on her hips. "I hoped the crew would get here early and help me set up a staging area, but there's an accident on Loop 12, and I've already gotten four texts telling me people are going to be late. Do you want to get changed while I set things up?"

"Let me help you," I said. "I'm much more comfortable moving furniture around than standing in front of a camera."

"I'd feel better if you rehearsed your lines. Did you prepare a script?"

"I have something in mind," I said vaguely.

"Good. I'm about to stir up some dust, which will make hair and makeup's job more difficult."

"Is hair and makeup necessary? I didn't realize we'd need them for a dry run."

"This isn't a dry run. We're filming all day." She pointed over her shoulder. "It'll take some time for the crew to set up the bounce screen and light fixtures, and we'll get it ready a lot faster if you stay out of my way. There's a card table set up out back with coffee and donuts. Help yourself."

I felt dismissed. Honestly, if she'd turned on her cameras and let me rearrange the furniture myself, it might have made for a decent commercial, but if she thought she was here for the public service announcement for the police, then my ideas wouldn't matter.

I left my garment bags where they were at the front of the store and went through the stockroom to the back exit. I was so lost in my thoughts that I stumbled over a sandbag that had fallen off a stack. After I regained my balance, I picked it up and placed it back on top of the stack. There was a hole on one corner, and sand spilled out onto the concrete floor.

I reached the exit and leaned on the door, but something blocked it on the other side. I pushed harder, jammed my foot in the opening, and eventually fit through.

And while I'd been too distracted by my thoughts to notice anything else, it was suddenly impossible to ignore the body of Olivia Jean, the original star of the commercial, lying on the ground outside the store, nor the brushed-aluminum coffee urn covered in blood beside her.

FIVE

A DARK RED STAIN MATTED OLIVIA'S TITIAN HAIR TO HER head. She was facedown, with her head turned to the side. Her arms were out on either side of her body. One of her long pink fingernails was missing from her left hand, making her fingers look distorted. I dropped to the ground and checked her wrist for a pulse. My handbag, with my phone, was inside the store, and the door had closed behind me. I called out for help, but I was in a parking lot to an abandoned place of business, and the only sign of life was the shiny black SUV parked next to the dumpster.

I stood, and my bad knee snapped, sending a spike of pain through my leg. The adrenaline rush of finding Olivia washed over me and minimized the pain. I moved as quickly as I could to the front of the store and reentered the building.

"Jules!" I called. It took a moment for my eyes to adjust to the interior after having been outside, and when shapes came into focus, I searched for my garment bag and hand-bag. Neither was where I'd left them. I kept my hands on the chairs along the aisle and moved toward the back. Jules wasn't there.

I closed my eyes and counted to five and then opened them. My vision improved to the point of being able to see. I called out for Jules two more times to no avail. The front door opened, and I whirled around and faced the silhouette of a hulking man carrying a long aluminum fixture in one hand and a handful of clamps in the other. The sun was behind him, and it was difficult to make out much more than that.

"Call the police," I demanded.

"Lady, chill out. I'm the key grip."

"There's a murdered woman out back, and I can't find my phone. Call the police!"

The man dropped the fixture. He pulled his phone out of his back pocket and held it out to me. I grabbed it and, faced with his lock screen, turned it back to him. The facial recognition unlocked it, and he handed it back. It felt like an hour had passed since I discovered Olivia's body, but it probably was less than five minutes.

I called 911, gave them my name, the address, and brief details of what I'd found. They instructed me and anyone else on the premises to stay there until the police arrived.

This was going to be some endorsement for the police.

I hung up the phone and handed it back to the man. Up close, I could see he had black hair, leathery skin, and square black glasses. He had tattoos up his arms and covering his neck, disappearing under an ill-fitting gray T-shirt. He put his phone into the back pocket of his jeans. My bad knee throbbed as it always did after a burst of adrenaline wore off, and I stretched my leg out in front of me and looked up at the man. "Thank you," I said.

"How'd you find her?" he asked.

"Jules told me to wait out back while she set up."

"Who's Jules?"

"The director."

"I thought Denton was the director."

"From what I understand, the police commissioner's wife wasn't happy with the way Olivia's commercial turned out and—" I stopped talking. Olivia was dead. Someone had killed her. And anything I said about Arlene's reaction to the commercial could be misconstrued.

Except...if Olivia was let go from the commercial reshoot, why had she been here today?

I forced myself to stand. "I'm Madison Night," I said. "Last night, I was asked to step in to film a commercial for the Lakewood Police. I didn't know Olivia was going to be here, but truth be told, the only details I was given were to show up by nine."

The man wore an oversized black utility watch strapped to his wrist with a band of black webbing, and he raised his arm and checked the time. "It's quarter after eight."

"I like to be early."

A beat of silence hung in the air. Finally, he introduced himself. "I'm Bruce," he said. "I oversee the light crew. You said the director's here?"

"Yes, but I don't know—" Again, I cut myself off. It

wouldn't help anyone for me to spread gossip, and right now, anything I said about Jules felt like exactly that.

A small door next to the checkout area opened toward us, and Jules came out. Her shirt was half tucked in, and she had her sunglasses back down over her eyes. "I thought you were going to wait outside," she said to me.

I stood. "Jules, there's been an accident." I didn't have a chance to say more because my voice was lost to the sirens of police cars that pulled into the lot out front.

I'D BEEN through enough scenes like this one to silently direct it myself. One uniformed officer remained inside the store with Jules and Bruce while I walked with the other one to show him where I'd found Olivia's body. He secured the area around her with yellow crime scene tape and asked me to wait inside. Two more SUVs pulled into the lot while we were behind the building, and the first officer on the scene met the arriving crew and told them to wait in their cars. If the call time was nine o'clock, then we'd have over a dozen people here within the next forty-five minutes, and that was going to be a difficult crowd to control. The chaotic crime scene aftermath had kept me distracted, but I still had no idea where my purse had gone. I walked around the perimeter of the store and reentered through the front door, where I found Ling Tsu and Sue Niedermeyer, the two Sues who worked homicide for Tex.

They saw me, and Ling, a thin Chinese woman with bone-straight black hair blunt cut to shoulder length, approached me. "Madison, I heard you made the call. Can you give me a statement?"

"Sure." I moved a few feet back to put distance between myself and Jules and Bruce and told Ling how the morning had unfolded. "Jules wanted to rearrange the furniture for the film shoot, and I went out back to have a cup of coffee. I went to the exit at the back of the stockroom. Someone blocked the door. When I eventually got it open, I found Olivia's body on the other side."

"What else did you see?"

"Exactly what you'll see when you go out there. Olivia's body is on the ground. There's blood matted in her hair and a coffee urn covered with blood not far away."

"What's your role here?" she asked, gesturing toward the interior of the store with her phone. "I mean, I know this place is right up your alley, but if you were helping Jules with the setup, then she wouldn't send you out back."

There was no avoiding this part. "Captain Allen and I were last-minute invites to a dinner party at the police commissioner's house last night. After viewing us the rough cut of the public service announcement for the Lakewood Police Department, the commissioner's wife convinced her husband to replace Olivia as the star of the commercials to promote the police department." I wasn't fond of saying this next part. "She suggested me as the replacement."

"You."

"Yes."

She switched off her phone. "What did Captain Allen say?"

"He wasn't thrilled with the idea."

She nodded as if she could imagine that. "Look, I know you know the drill, but you're the person who found the body. Can you tell me anything else? Did you see anything suspicious?"

"There's a stack of sandbags inside the back door. One of them has a hole in it, and there's sand scattered across the floor. I stepped in it before going outside and probably tracked some sand with me. If someone else went that way first, they would have tracked sand too."

Ling made a call. "Do you see any sand around the body?" she asked. "Keep looking." She hung up.

I glanced past Ling to where Sue was interviewing Bruce. He peered over her head at where Ling and I conversed. I already knew Ling and Sue were skilled interrogators. If Bruce had something to hide, it would come out. But everything I'd noticed about this situation was conjecture. It was the kind of information that could put a person in the crosshairs of an investigation, and I'd learned through experience that often, the person identified as the most viable candidate early on inspired a sort of tunnel vision in the investigators. It was an effective strategy for when they were right, but I'd seen them not be right before.

My duty to the police was to give them an accurate statement, so I told Ling what I could. "I refused this opportunity twice. I finally relented because of the chance to go through this abandoned furniture store."

"You've never been here before?" Ling asked. She looked around. "That's hard to believe."

"I never knew it existed. Arlene Fraleigh told me about the place last night."

Ling made a note and then prompted me to continue.

"I arrived early because I was curious about the store, but I think Jules—the director—expected to have some uninterrupted time to set things up the way she wanted before the crew got here."

"Was she here when you arrived?"

"Yes."

"Do you know how long?"

"No. When she asked me to wait out back, she told me she brought donuts and coffee for the crew."

Ling held up her index finger and made another call. "Is there a box of donuts out back?" she asked. "Just coffee?" She watched me and waited and then nodded. "From where?" She nodded again. "Okay." She hung up, turned the voice recorder app back on, and asked me, "Anything else?"

"I stumbled over the sandbag and then put it on the stack and tried to leave. The back exit door wouldn't open. I forced it open with my weight and found Olivia's body on the ground. I called out to Jules for help, but the door closed behind me, and I doubt she could hear. My handbag with my phone was inside, so I came back around the building. Bruce," I pointed to the muscular man, "arrived before I located my phone. That's why the phone call came from his number."

"Okay. If you remember anything else, give me a call." She pulled a card out of her pocket and handed it to me. "Formality." She dropped her phone in her pocket.

I took the card and curled my fingers around it. Ling rejoined Sue, and the two of them conferred while it dawned on me that Ling's interest in the donuts had nothing to do with stereotypical police behavior.

It had to do with the donuts themselves. Because while Jules had offered me coffee and donuts, only the coffee urn had been present outside. But why would a killer take the donuts?

SIX

I WASN'T SURPRISED WHEN LING SAID OUR FILMING LOCATION was off-limits for the foreseeable future. To the crew, it must have been a letdown, but to me, it felt like a sign. One by one, the people who arrived to work on the police commercial gave their contact information to Jules and then left. I remained behind; I couldn't leave until I found my keys.

I was hesitant to make a friendly connection with Jules. She had revealed that she'd been the assistant director for the upcoming movie about my life, but she hadn't mentioned her engagement to Hudson. It was possible he hadn't revealed our history to her. I'd already heard that the screenwriters had taken liberties with the facts to create a more box-office-ready movie, and it was possible my relationship with Hudson had been reduced to a professional one. The best way to avoid drama at this point was to keep my distance.

After the last of the crew left, Jules approached me.

"Madison, I put your clothes and handbag in the restroom," she said. "We're the only two women on the set, and I assumed that's where you'd change."

"Oh. Yes. That makes sense. Where's the restroom?"

She pointed to the door alongside the register. It was the door she exited from when I was talking to Bruce, which answered my earlier question about where she'd been.

"Thank you." I approached Ling and Sue, who were conversing in low voices a few feet away. "Excuse me for interrupting. I just learned my personal belongings were moved to the powder room by the register, and I need my handbag before I leave. May I take it, or do you need to see the room first?"

They exchanged glances, and then Sue looked at me. "It sure is nice to work with someone who understands our job."

I led Sue to the powder room and stood by the door while she entered, cued up the video app on her phone, and filmed the interior while she slowly pivoted in a circle. She closed the door between us, and I waited out front for about a minute. She reopened the door and handed me my garment bag and purse.

"Open them for me," she said.

I set the garment bag on the chair on the end and unsnapped the closure on my handbag. I held it open so Sue could see the interior. She wore black rubber gloves and shifted my personal belongings around the interior to check the contents. She nodded. I set my purse down and unzipped the garment bag. The jacket to the fur-trimmed suit was missing from its hanger. I held the bag up and stuck my hand into the bottom, feeling around for it, but the only thing there was a pouch filled with costume jewelry options.

"There's a jacket missing," I said. "It's ivory tweed trimmed in fox fur."

"You're sure you brought it?"

I thought back to earlier this morning when I removed the pink mock turtleneck and matching pants from the bag and how my hand had brushed against the collar. "I'm certain it was in there."

"Do me a favor. When you get home, check your closet to make sure you don't have it. Call me or Ling when you know."

I agreed. It was a small detail, but it bothered me. I knew the jacket had been in the garment bag when I packed up from the first shoot, and I'd been so let down by the commercial filming process that I'd simply hung the garment bag in my closet and grabbed it today. I doubted the jacket could have fallen out without me noticing, but that troubled me too. If I hadn't misplaced it in the past twenty-four hours, then someone had taken it. The questions, once I confirmed my absentmindedness wasn't to blame, were when and why.

Sue and Ling permitted me to leave. I walked to my car and double-checked the back seat and the trunk first and then started the engine and backed out of my space. I felt someone's eyes on me and looked around, spotting Bruce by the back of the building, a few feet from where I'd found Olivia's body. I gave him a half-hearted wave and left.

Most people would assume the finding of a body would shoot an entire day, but I wasn't most people. Five months ago, I'd been approved for a business expansion loan from a local bank. I'd been through legal troubles prior to that and had spent an embarrassing month or two waffling between failure and lack of direction. It had been a vacant commercially zoned property next to my house that relit the fuse to my motivation, along with some public shaming from a college professor. The bank approved the loan with the co-signature of Donna Nast, a thirty-something bombshell who had so many former identities she was like a cat with nine lives. The difference was that Nasty, I believed, would outlive the scrappiest feline.

Nasty made it clear she wasn't my business partner, but we both knew there was no way I'd allow myself to default on a loan with her as the cosigner. I'd come a long way since seeing her as my nemesis, but I still didn't like the tilted power balance that existed between us. She agreed to monthly status reports on my business expansion, and now that my afternoon was cleared, I drove to my office to update my profit-and-loss statement for our next meeting.

The primary office for Mad for Mod was in a storefront on Greenville Avenue. After losing everything but my decorating license in a legal battle, I used half of the business loan to aggressively pursue inventory for future projects. I called on satisfied clients to help spread word of mouth about my specialty—mid-century modern design, self-taught from studying sets in Doris Day movies—and I spent the months of November through January in a blur of redecorating bathrooms, home offices, and dens. I signed up for weekend courses on laying tile and refinishing floors, and I'd even earned income from the city for designing a holiday display on Elm Street outside of the pajama factory I had inherited a few years ago and converted to office space.

Since losing everything provides the unique opportunity to rebuild things the way you wanted them in the first place, I'd torn down the storage locker in my lot and added two additional parking spaces.

I parked next to a small white Mini Cooper. My first order of business expansion had been to contact my lone employee, Effie Jones, and offer her a salaried job. Effie was still learning the basics of mid-century design, but she was a whiz with a spreadsheet, and cataloging inventory lit her up in a way I'd not known possible. She accepted my offer, gave two weeks' notice at the Waffle House, where her business degree was going to waste (waist?), and took charge, leaving me free to focus on new clients, new inventory, and new ideas.

Effie was at her desk in the office. "Celebrity decorator in the house!" she called out when she saw me.

Ever since my first commercial aired, I'd gained a new level of fame that my involvement in a number of homicides around town had not given me. Even the owner of the paint store I frequented called to say sales of the line of paints I'd endorsed had sold out after months of collecting dust, and he'd had to reorder twice. Effie, being of an age that was fascinated with fame, was thrilled with this turn of events. She'd tried to convince me to use my new platform to launch a social media campaign, but I'd reminded her the point of being a decorator was to decorate.

"How'd the commercial go? I thought you were going to send me a link to the rough cut."

"There's been a complication." I set my handbag on my desk, opened it, and pulled out the white envelope filled with cash. I pulled Drew Billings's business card out of the envelope and handed both to Effie. "Can you contact this man and arrange to return this money?"

Effie took both and looked in the envelope. "Boss, this is cash. Did you finally sell the sailboat you acquired in December? I thought you'd get about five hundred for that. Where'd you find a buyer?"

"It's not from the boat," I said. "I was approached to film a commercial for the police, but I don't think it's in the cards."

Effie set the envelope down. "Hold up," she said. "You said your commercial was bad, but if that's true, then why would they give you—" She thumbed through the envelope — "ten thousand dollars in cash?"

I pulled the second envelope out of my handbag and handed it to her. "Twenty thousand. And I didn't say it was bad. And how do you know that's ten thousand dollars?"

"I know what ten thousand dollars looks like."

Of course she did. She was from the Instagram generation, and if popular hashtags were any indication, her age group was expert in both conspicuous consumption and saving the environment. She could probably look at a picture of a landfill and accurately guess the number of discarded laundry detergent bottles.

I filled Effie in on how I'd come to be offered the job and why it was a moot point. "Once word gets out that the former spokesperson was murdered on the set of the police department commercial, Commissioner Fraleigh is going to have a real publicity nightmare on his hands."

"Do you think that's why she was murdered? To hurt the police's reputation?"

I rested on the edge of my desk and faced Effie. "I suppose it's possible. But it seems a roundabout way to hurt them. Olivia wasn't an actor by trade. She was a dancer at Jumbos."

Effie's eyes went wide. "Captain Allen hired a *stripper?*"

"Captain Allen had nothing to do with it," said a male voice from the front of the showroom. The voice was followed with comingled barks and yips, then two dogs rounded the corner and entered the office. Rocky put his paws on my knees, and Wojo went straight to his water bowl. A moment later, Tex entered my office.

SEVEN

TEX WORE THE SAME SUIT HE'D HAD ON LAST NIGHT. HE'D loosened the tie around his neck and opened the button by the collar of his shirt. He held a plastic grocery store bag with something lumpy inside. He looked ready for happy hour, and it wasn't yet noon. The news of Olivia's death had reached him.

"The original commercial shoot was written, cast, and produced by Edward Fraleigh's team," Tex said. "I never wanted a commercial. I suggested a different direction."

"Sock hop?" I asked.

"Barbecue," Tex answered.

"Sometimes you two speak your own language," Effie grumbled.

Tex and I shared a conspiratorial smile before his face grew serious. "Can I talk to you alone for a moment?"

"Sure." I hopped down from the desk and turned to Effie. "Call Mr. Billings, okay?"

She nodded.

Tex stepped back and let me exit the office first.

I grabbed Rocky's rope bone and headed to a quiet corner of my showroom. The dogs followed. I tossed the favorite toy from Rocky's puppy years onto the carpet square by the front door, and he attacked it. Wojo stood by, watching, occasionally crouching down as if preparing to join in the battle against the colorful braided enemy.

I sat in a low Finn Juhl Pelican chair. It was navy blue with red buttons tufted into the back, and the curve of the chair embraced me like a hug from behind. The chair was unique thanks to its surrealistic proportions. The short oak legs brought my center of gravity lower to the ground than usual, and I felt like I was on the Island of Lilliput. I wrapped my arms around my knees and waited for Tex.

I thought Tex was right behind me, but it took a few minutes for him to appear. Instead of sitting down, he stood in front of me and held his hands out. I took them, and he pulled me to my feet. He wrapped me in a close embrace and whispered in my ear. "You okay?"

I nodded. This was a different response from where we'd been in the past, and I liked it. Tex relaxed his arms, stepped back, and looked me square in the eyes. "Walk me through your morning."

"I should have known the consolation window would be short."

"C'mon, Night, don't I get a little credit for that?"

I smiled and then lowered myself back into my chair. Tex sat in the Pelican chair opposite me and rearranged himself a few times before giving up and sticking his feet out in front of him. "You chose these chairs on purpose."

"Maybe."

This time, he smiled. We were gradually finding ways to exist in each other's lives, contrasting as they were.

"I went to Fraleigh Furniture after my morning swim. It was around eight. That's earlier than I was supposed to arrive, but I wanted some time alone to mentally prepare."

In the background, I could hear the dogs snarling as they engaged in a game of tug-of-war with the rope bone. "Like a dog with a bone" was an expression for a reason.

Tex held up his hand. "This was all just a vague idea last night at the party. How'd you end up at Fraleigh Furniture today?"

"Drew Billings was waiting for me at the pool."

Tex's expression hardened. He crossed his arms, and his eyes narrowed.

"He offered me an envelope of cash to film your commercial and hinted that I could use the same crew to refilm my commercial as well. The whole thing was set up to take place at the Fraleigh store. It was one carrot dangled in front of another. I could hardly say no."

Tex didn't waste time confirming the obvious. Telling me about a store of mid-century furniture that had been sitting untouched for fifty years was like waving a red flag in front of a bull.

"How much did Billings offer you?"

"Twenty thousand dollars. Isn't that a bit much for a city office?"

"Talent isn't cheap."

"What were you paying Olivia?"

"More." He scratched his arm. "Where's the money?"

"I gave it to Effie and told her to arrange to return it. If there's not going to be a commercial, then it doesn't seem right to keep the money."

"Hold on to it for now." Tex leaned back and rested his hands on his thighs. The curvature of the back of the Pelican chair wrapped around his upper arms, and if the legs of the chair had been a foot taller, I'd have said he might find the seating option comfortable.

So far, Tex hadn't asked me to tell him about finding Olivia's body, and I assumed he'd gotten my statement from Ling. But one detail hadn't come up that morning, and I felt it might be important to share.

"Did Ling or Sue talk to the director this morning?"

"Denton Gold? Neither one of them mentioned him."

"Denton was replaced with a woman. Her name is Jules. She was at the store when I got there, and she's the one who told me to wait out back. If I hadn't, I don't know how long it would have been until someone discovered Olivia's body."

Tex's eyes narrowed. "Do you have some reason to suspect her?"

"Quite the contrary. I'm fairly sure Jules is Hudson's fiancée."

Tex's expression went through a couple of emotions, and I recognized surprise, curiosity, and suspicion among them. Suspicion was the one that lingered, and it was aimed at me. "Hudson's engaged?"

I nodded. "He's moved on from his life here. She worked on his movie. She was here in Dallas to film establishing shots. That's how they met. She knows who I am in terms of the story of that case, but I don't know if she knows about my history with him."

"Wouldn't that come out in the movie?"

"I got the feeling the screenwriters took liberties with the source material."

He nodded and appeared to chew on that for a moment. "What's she like?"

It was an unexpected question, but I gave Tex the benefit of the doubt and assumed it related to the case. "She's younger than me. Mid- to late thirties, I'd guess. She seems nice, though I didn't spend a lot of time talking to her. She was arranging the furniture for the shoot when I got there. I offered to help, but she asked me to wait outside."

"You said she was the director? She shouldn't be the one doing the heavy lifting."

"I could be wrong, but I think she got there early for the same reason I did. She wanted to get things ready her way before the crew arrived. Me showing up before I was expected seemed to unsettle her."

He nodded. "What's your gut tell you about her?"

This was a delicate question. My life felt inextricably tied to Hudson and Tex thanks to the case on which we met, and Hudson's choice to sell the rights to that story had cemented it as a moment in time that would live in perpetuity. My first response when I'd been face to face with Jules was that she was young. I was genuinely happy for Hudson, but it was difficult not to go down the road of one-of-these-things-is-not-like-the-other.

"She was nonthreatening. I know that's vague, but the

short amount of time I spent with her gave me the impression that she was there to do a job, she knew she was inheriting someone else's crew, and she was nervous. She was aloof but not standoffish. It seemed to bother her when I offered to help move the furniture, but if she knew who I was, then she should know I've moved more furniture in my lifetime than most."

"Did she say anything about Olivia?"

"I don't think she ever heard of Olivia. I can't imagine she sent me out back for coffee so I could stumble over a body. Especially if she was responsible for it."

Tex nodded. That was the thing. There was something off about Jules in the moment, but sending me directly on the path that led to finding Olivia's body was too convenient. A murderer would want to keep their crime hidden, not exposed.

"Jules told me she brought coffee and donuts. When I saw Olivia, it was obvious someone struck her on the head. A bloody coffee urn sat on the ground nearby, and I assume that was the murder weapon. I'm sure your lab will run tests to prove it."

"But?"

"But the donuts were missing. If this had been a heat-of-the-moment attack and someone grabbed the urn to strike Olivia, then why would they take the donuts?"

Tex sat back in his chair. His clear blue eyes were on mine, and I could practically hear the wheels turning in his brain. He leaned forward, bent his knees, and propped his elbows on his thighs. "Ninety percent of the world connects donuts to cops."

"I do remember, when Jules mentioned them, thinking we could use them as a prop in the commercial," I said with a wry smile. "The goal of your campaign is to soften the image of the police and get people to trust you again. Running with the stereotype, especially if done correctly, is going to humanize you."

"Do you think that's why Jules brought them?"

"No, I think she brought them because she passed a donut shop on her way to the furniture store, and she thought it was a cheap way to bribe the crew."

Tex studied me for a moment, and I knew from experience it was because he was processing information.

Tex reached down to the plastic bag by his feet and pulled out a familiar garment. It was soiled beyond recognition and smelled of motor oil and sugar. If not for the amber-tipped fox-fur trim, I would have assumed it was a rag.

"Sue found this half a mile from the furniture factory. Do you recognize it?"

"It's mine," I said. "I packed it as a potential outfit to wear for the commercial." I reached forward, and he pulled it away.

"Sorry, Night. It's evidence. Besides, I'm not sure there's a cleaner in town who can bring it back to life."

I waved my hand in front of my nose. "What's on it?"

"Motor oil. Found an empty jug a few feet away."

"Why would someone pour motor oil on my vintage jacket?"

He dropped the jacket into the plastic bag. "We found

your jacket wrapped around a crushed pink bakery box filled with fresh donuts."

I considered what this meant. "Does that tell you anything?"

"It narrows the timeline. Olivia's murder happened after you arrived."

EIGHT

IMMEDIATELY, I FOLLOWED TEX'S TRAIN OF THOUGHT. MY jacket arrived at the store with me—or had it? "I had that jacket with me at the airplane hangar yesterday. And at the pool this morning. It could have been taken at either of those times or places, and I wouldn't have known."

"You said Billings approached you at the pool?"

"Right," I said. "But it's a woman's vintage fur-trimmed tweed jacket. And it's March. Not the first choice of someone who wants to blend into a crowd."

"We'll run tests on it and see if we can pull any DNA, but the motor oil probably broke down any trace evidence that was there."

I understood the futile nature of what Tex suggested. Whoever had killed Olivia had taken the donuts. My jacket being wrapped around the box meant my jacket had come in contact with the killer too. The presence of motor oil indicated the killer tried to destroy anything that could lead back to him or her, but ditching the jacket, the donuts, and the empty motor oil container so close to the crime scene had been sloppy.

What was still unclear was why Olivia had been at the new film site in the first place. If I'd been hired to replace her, then she'd been relieved of her contract. The filming site had changed, so even if she showed up for work, why would she show up at Fraleigh Furniture?

Tex interrupted my thoughts. "I have a big ask," he said. "You're free to say no."

I held my hand up. "I'm just getting my business back on the ground. Please don't ask me to do anything to compromise the plans I already have set into motion. You know how important Mad for Mod is to me."

"I've got another trip this weekend. Ling and Sue are running point on this one, but the commissioner's pressuring us to act fast. I want you to film the commercial. Use the same crew. I'll get the crime scene cleared so you can go back tomorrow. I need eyes on the inside, and as much as it pains me to say it, you're ideal."

"Is this why you told me to hold onto the money from Billings?" I asked.

He raised one eyebrow but didn't say anything. I'd never expected Tex to ask me for a favor like this and was prepared to dig in my heels, but this troubled me on a different level.

"One of the crew members could be the killer," I said.

"You won't be in danger. I'll hire private security to be present the entire time, and I'll get my people there too. You might recognize a few faces, but I need you to play along with their covers. Can you do that?"

"Sure," I said. My confidence level didn't match my voice, which proved the ability to act did lie within me. "How do you want to play this?"

"I'll make arrangements before I leave. If I get everything lined up, you'll be back to shooting tomorrow. If I'm right and this is about the police, then someone's going to be unhappy that the commercial is still being made."

"What if this isn't about the police? What if it's about Olivia?"

"I'll get the two Sues to dig into her background and find out if she did anything that put a target on her back."

AFTER TEX LEFT WITH WOJO, I led Rocky to the office. He curled up in his dog bed and proceeded to fall asleep. I touched base with Effie. "Did you call Drew Billings?"

"I tried. He didn't answer, and his mailbox is full. I left a message with Edward Fraleigh's office. Do you want me to go to his office?"

"No. Let's put a pin in that and move on to business. I've got a meeting with Nasty next week, and I'd like to update her on the profit-and-loss statement."

"Sure, Boss."

Back when I first rented my showroom, the office had been exclusively for me. I'd discovered one important thing since then: I don't work well with a chatty millennial by my side. I took inspiration from the bakery that had their pastry chef work in the window to attract sidewalk traffic and set my office up in the front of the studio, where people on the street could see me digging through swatch books, creating vision boards, and sketching out concepts. My other office, at the new property by my house, was more private, and I split my time between the two locations depending on my workload.

After my commercial aired, my calendar filled with consultations, but an unplanned termite infestation at a client's property had caused a last-minute cancellation in the middle of March. Since relaunching my business, I tried to keep busy with either new business or ideas for expansion. I'd decorated every spare inch of my house and had it professionally photographed for my portfolio of work, but I still felt there was more I could do. I was already prepared for a client appointment at six tonight, so I let my mind wander to what else I could renovate to use as an example for potential clients.

Until Tex entered my life, all the renovations and decorations at Thelma Johnson's house had been for me: the yellow kitchen, the wall of sunburst clocks that lost time at varying intervals in the living room, and the daisy-covered sheets on the bed. I'd decorated a room in Tex's townhouse once and still had the keys, but sneaking in and redecorating his personal space without permission felt passive-aggressive, not generous.

Tex had been working as much as I had, spending weeks at a time on the road to visit universities and recruit for the Lakewood PD. Dating a homicide detective made it difficult to pull off surprises, but now that the worst of my business troubles were behind me, I wanted to expand. If there were something I could do that Tex would appreciate as much as me, that would be best, and if I could do it in secret, even better. But where could I decorate that he wouldn't see?

The garage. The idea hit me from out of the blue. Thelma Johnson's property had a freestanding garage that sat by the back of the plot of land. Now, what could I do with the garage?

A woodshop?

I'd already installed a shed with tools on the property and spent a weekend weatherproofing it. Besides, woodworking wasn't Tex's passion. He'd managed a few tasks for me, but compared to Hudson's expert skills as a handyman, Tex's had fallen short. I neither wanted nor needed him to fill those shoes. I'd been taking classes on the side to learn how to handle small jobs myself, and anything I couldn't do, I could hire out.

An indoor shooting range?

That set a bad precedent. One time, Tex had been so frustrated with a case that he took aim at a gnarled oak tree in my backyard. A neighbor chastised him from a second-story window, revealing that this wasn't the first time. But as a police captain, he had access to an indoor range to requalify and practice, and that should be enough. When he was here, I wanted him to relax.

As I considered the options, I flipped through the mess of paperwork in my inbox and came across a glossy, over-sized postcard from another local business owner: Jimmy's Pools of Dallas. I'd kept it as a reminder to consider a direct mail campaign for Mad for Mod, but after relegating it to my inbox, I'd forgotten all about it. Until today.

I slid the postcard out from the pile and stared at the

image. It advertised an in-ground, fiberglass pool installed in one week. I pulled up the corresponding website and scanned the details while my mind buzzed. I'd never considered decorating outdoor spaces, but why not? This was Dallas. Houses with backyard pools were a dime a dozen around here. I couldn't believe I'd never thought of this before.

A few houses in my neighborhood had installed pools, and the idea of being able to go out back and relax in the water after a long day was delightful. Now that I'd expanded my real estate holding to include the commercial property next to my house, I wasn't looking to move any time soon.

My imagination ran wild. I'd never designed a pool before, and that made this, a pool on my property, doubly special. It would increase the property value and give me an entirely new set of concepts to include in my portfolio.

I spent the rest of the afternoon going through back issues of *Atomic Ranch* magazine, looking for inspiration, finding plenty in the recent Palm Springs issue. We'd need lounge chairs and a patio umbrella. A shaded cabana area for people like me who preferred to remain out of the sun. I could install a firepit for backyard cookouts and perhaps even a tiki bar. The only question left was how to install a pool in secret, but with Tex's recruiting commitments and this latest case, the timing was opportune.

Before I changed my mind, I called Jimmy's Pools of Dallas.

NINE

"HELLO, THIS IS MADISON NIGHT. I'M A LOCAL DECORATOR, and I'm interested in a swimming pool."

"Madison Night?" repeated a male voice. "Are you that decorator I've been seeing on the TV?"

"I very well may be," I replied.

"I'm Jimmy. My kids like your commercial. I've got an eleven-year-old daughter and she started wearing her grandmother's daisy pin after she saw you. Is this for a client?"

"No, it's for me. I have a freestanding garage on the corner of my property, and I'd like to have it replaced with a pool."

"Let me pull up the calendar. Looks like the soonest I can go is the end of April. I'm booked solid from May to September. What were you thinking?"

"I was hoping for something sooner."

"How much sooner?"

"Tomorrow?" I said, my voice raising to turn the word into a question. Jimmy chuckled. I added, "You said you've seen my commercial, so you know I'm in the process of expanding my business. If I can get it installed now, I can decorate the outdoor space, have it photographed, and possibly drum up additional business over the summer. You'll get full credit for the pool work, of course."

"I love your enthusiasm, but I'm not the one you need to convince. Ever since the pandemic, there aren't enough laborers to do the demolition work. My team could be out at daybreak, but if you don't have a hole in the ground, there's not much we can do."

Not long ago, I'd spent some time at a local college in pursuit of a business degree. That experience had taught me to open my eyes and see opportunity in challenge.

"Jimmy, I have an idea. Can you give me a moment?"

"Sure."

I put Jimmy on hold and did a quick internet search for excavators. The price was in line with the cost of installing a pool. The biggest lesson I'd learned while in business school was that there was no reward without risk, so I took a bolstering breath and returned to the phone call.

"I have a proposition for you."

Effie approached me and set our profit-and-loss statement on my desk. I saw the balance owed on the loan and knew the best way to pay off the balance was to expedite my expansion. "I'll buy you an excavator in exchange for the pool. You'll have the necessary equipment to keep demolition in-house."

"The excavator plus cost of materials," he countered.

"How about the excavator plus world-of-mouth advertising to my client database and I'll share the rights to images from a professional photo shoot of the completed project with you. What do you say?"

The other end of the phone was silent. I clicked the receiver a few times and then said, "Hello? Are you still there?"

"Lady, you got yourself a deal."

I explained to Jimmy the clandestine nature of the pool installation. He had a few interesting ideas of his own, and I admired his ability to think outside the box. We established a seven-day window for installation. I gave him my address so he could take measurements and advise me on the best way to proceed, and I arranged the purchase of a mini Bobcat excavator against my line of credit from a local dealer while we were still on the phone. Green lights ahead.

After I hung up, I prepared for my evening client appointment. The house in question was a single-family home in the Hillridge neighborhood. It had originally been built in 1969 with desirable mid-century bones, but an ill-advised previous owner had gutted all original elements of the house and replaced them with generic features designed to appeal to the masses.

When I first met with Paulie and Paolo Mangieri, the same-sex couple who bought the house for themselves and their two adopted children, I knew everything would be okay. They were my first private-residence client after reopening my decorating business, and we'd bonded over an original American Standard bathtub in the obscure shade Orchid of Vincennes that was up for grabs outside a local house on trash day. The shared passion for colorful bathroom fixtures was so unexpected that we both almost lost rights to the fixture when the homeowner came out of his house and told us to keep down the noise. Turned out he had a matching toilet, sink, and seven boxes of unused tile still inside his garage, which he allowed Paulie and Paolo to have for the low price of getting off his property.

A fifteen-hundred-square-foot ranch house was a dream for mid-mod enthusiasts, and the Mangieris were no different. They bought the house knowing it would require restoration and had relished the idea of tackling the work themselves. But then Paolo got a job at a bakery, and Paulie hurt his back laying tile in the bathroom, and the idea of DIY restoration became less attractive. They hired a team of contractors to finish the projects they'd started, and then fate intervened in the form of an orchid bathtub. Bing, bam, boom.

I may have lost the battle, but not the fight, because by the time I returned to my showroom, there was a message on my machine asking for a consultation. One week later, they hired me to design an in-home ice cream parlor.

Tonight, I needed a distraction. And I could think of no distraction better than this. The couple had decided to convert the breakfast nook into a novelty space for the family to enjoy. Their house had a surprising amount of interior space for a home from the sixties, and with two kids under six, they knew the timing was right to choose whimsy over elegance. I'd been to the house twice to take pictures and had a design direction I hoped they'd love. I was in the process of outsourcing the materials needed to make it work on their budget, which meant afternoons stalking Craigslist and Facebook Marketplace.

I collected two colorful concept boards and slid them into a flat zippered drafting bag that I'd obtained in an estate sale buyout of Mark Baker, an engineer for a local airplane parts factory. Along with the drafting bag, I'd acquired over a hundred cardboard tubes with schematics for propellers, engines, and landing gear and the world's largest collection of men's short-sleeved dress shirts.

I zipped the portfolio closed and exited my computer windows, then went to find Effie in the office. It was after six, though I'd found Effie preferred to stick around and work after hours.

"Hey, Boss," she said.

Rocky lifted his furry head and looked at me then lowered his head and closed his eyes again.

"Do you want me to email Nasty the documents ahead of time, or do you want to take a copy for her?"

I almost felt bad that Effie had adopted my (and everybody else's) nickname for Nasty. "Email and tell her we can review them when we meet. Let her know it's up to her if she prints a copy. I prefer not to have documents of a financial nature floating around in the world."

"Got it." She clicked a few more times and then typed something brief. "Done." The girl was a marvel of technological efficiency. She glanced at the zippered folio. "Is that for the Mangieris? Are you headed there now?"

"I'm taking the concept boards. They think tonight is for

measurements. I thought I'd surprise them. Clients appreciate being kept in the loop along the way."

"Makes sense." She leaned down and picked up a plastic bag by her feet. "I found these at Trader's Village and thought you might want to use them." She handed me the bag.

I peeked inside and saw several sealed bundles of pink-and-white-striped paper straws in unopened plastic packaging.

"These are great!"

"I know, right?" she said. She was pleased by my response. "There's more where they came from. I can go back and buy them out if you want."

"I haven't been out to Trader's Village for a while," I said. The light in her eyes dimmed a little. "Take money from petty cash and buy up as many as they have."

Her smile returned.

I said good night and headed for the back door. The phone jingled as I put my hand on the knob, and I turned and headed back to the office in the event it was for me. The phone in question was my yellow donut phone, and Effie held the curved receiver to her head and made eye contact, holding up her index finger and nodding. "Yes, I understand. I'll give her the message." She hung up and stared at me with her eyes wide. "That was Mr. Fraleigh. He said he was returning the message I left about Mr. Billings."

I chewed my lower lip and considered how to play off my offer to return the money now that Tex had asked me to follow through with the job.

"I don't think you have to worry about giving back the

money," she said as if reading my mind. "Commissioner Fraleigh said Drew Billings is no longer on his payroll." She picked up the envelopes of cash and extended them toward me. "He knew nothing of a cash advance but was adamant that he still wanted you on the commercial."

Hmmm. That wasn't suspicious at *all*.

TEN

I RECALLED THE LOOK ON TEX'S FACE WHEN I FIRST TOLD HIM about the money and how he suggested I keep it. Instinct directed me to hold out my hand for the envelope even though what Effie said made no sense. "Drew Billings was at the dinner party last night when Arlene told me about her store. He came to the pool with the money this morning and instructed me when and where to show up. That message doesn't make sense."

"Do you want me to call him back? Maybe I misunderstood."

"No, leave it. I changed my mind about the commercial anyway. I'm sure I'll have a chance to find out the details on the set."

I consolidated the cash and put the envelope in my handbag. It was too late to take it to a teller window at the bank, and I wasn't yet comfortable depositing this much money into an ATM. I clipped Rocky's leash to his collar, said good night a second time, and left.

It was a five-mile drive to the Mangieri residence, but traffic along Dallas neighborhood streets made this the worst time of the day to make the trip. My five miles took thirty-three minutes, and by the time I pulled into the long driveway that led to their property, I realized how long it had been since I ate.

The Mangieris were fans of Rocky, as was their Scottish fold cat, Connery. I parked my car and held Rocky's leash while I eased the leather folio out from behind the driver's seat and approached the front door.

Thankfully, the previous owner hadn't touched the exterior of the Mangieri house. The left half was almost solidly white brick, with one lone window interrupting the façade. The right half was recessed about ten feet back from the left, and the front door was at the spot where the left and right met. To the right of the front door was a large picture window accented by a diagonal grid of panes. Once a landscaper removed the overgrown shrubs that concealed the bottom third of the window, it would give the house real curb appeal.

The front door opened before I had a chance to ring the bell. I jumped, and Paulie Mangieri greeted me with a laugh. "Ha!" he said. "You thought you were going to surprise us, but we surprised you, didn't we?" Paulie was a white man with a shaved head and a shadow of a beard. He had mischievous wide-set blue eyes and dimples on display when he smiled, which was often. He held Connery in one hand and scratched the cat's striped gray head. "Your office called with a message." He shifted Connery so the cat's paws were over his shoulder. "You are to arrive on set, camera ready, by eight o'clock." He held out a piece of paper with handwritten notes. "Follow me. We have much to discuss."

Paulie turned around, leaving me face to face with the cat. Connery, however, had his eyes trained on Rocky. He clawed his way over Paulie's shoulder and hopped onto a nearby counter then to a chair then to the floor. Rocky strained his leash to get closer, and I tightened my grip.

"I wanted to surprise you with some illustrations for the—"

Paulie held up his hand to cut me off. "Little ears," he said. He nodded his head back and to the side to indicate two kids watching TV from the sofa. Maggie, the four-year-old, pushed herself down from the sofa, ran over to me, and threw her arms around my legs.

I put my hand on her head. "Hi, Maggie," I said. I glanced up at Paulie's face and then at Rocky. He nodded. "Would you like to play with Rocky?" I asked the girl.

Andy climbed down and ran over to join us. "Hi, Rocky!" he said. He dropped to the floor and stroked the dog's head. "Can I unclip him from his leash, Dad?"

Paulie looked at me, and this time, I nodded. Andy unclipped the leash, and Rocky raced into the hallway after Connery. The kids giggled and ran after them, leaving me alone with the person I'd come to see in the first place.

Paulie led me to the dining room, where we sat catty-corner from each other at seats by the end of the table. I set the folio down and unzipped it. "I thought you'd like to see the concepts for your new room." I slid the mat boards out and pushed them toward Paulie. Paint chips and material samples were affixed to the surface.

Paulie turned them in his direction and held the colorful compilations as far away from his face as his arm would allow then slipped a pair of glasses from the pocket of his shirt and put them on. He assessed the illustration again, this time holding it at a reasonable distance from his face. He picked up another one in his right hand and studied it too. I'd been expecting cheers of appreciation for what I'd imagined and planned, but his silence set my nerves on edge. Had I missed the mark?

Paulie pushed himself away from the table and left the room. By this time, my heart was thumping aggressively and despite the cool temperature, I felt damp under my arms. I'd never had a client storm out of a room before.

He returned with Paolo. He was a chubby Italian with an excitable nature. He had unruly black hair, a perpetual five o'clock shadow, and a smile that could light up a baseball stadium. Paulie pointed to the images, and Paolo rubbed his eyes and then leaned on the table and stared down at the concept boards. I swallowed a lump in my throat and folded my hands in my lap. Perhaps there was a reason the Mangieris had burned through so many decorators before me.

Paolo looked at Paulie, who nodded. Paolo turned to me, yanked me out of my chair, and threw his arms around me in an unexpected bear hug. He pinned my arms to my sides with his strong embrace, and I stood there not sure what was going on.

Paolo finally released me and moved his hands to my

upper arms. He pulled me close and kissed one cheek and then the other. *"Bellissimo!"* he said. He beamed broadly.

The sudden burst of enthusiasm took me by surprise, and I looked back and forth between Paulie and Paolo's faces. "To be clear, you like the design concept, right?"

"We no like," Paolo said. The men exchanged smiles and then laughed together. "We *love!*"

We filled the next forty minutes with questions and answers about the design. I'd planned to drop off the folio and leave them to their evening, but they would hear nothing of it. I walked them through what I'd conceived of and suggested features and storage options. Their enthusiasm matched mine, and I couldn't wait to get started.

At one point, Paolo left the room. I filled Paulie in on my day, and Paolo returned with a tray of espresso and fresh biscotti. Paolo was a pastry chef at a local Italian bakery, and despite the late hour, there was no way I was turning down something he'd made.

"Madison's been holding out on us," Paulie said to Paolo. He looked at me and continued. "She has a call time of eight o'clock Monday morning. She's expected to be camera-ready."

Paolo assembled a piece of fig biscotti on a plate and handed it to me. "What is this, a film? You act in addition to design?"

"Hardly," I said. Now that my strengths had been appreciated, it was easy to confess my shortcomings. "I recorded a commercial myself, low production value shot with my phone, and it's brought in enough leads to keep me busy. And through an unfortunate set of circumstances, I've been retained to also film a testimonial for the local police. I'm supposed to work with a crew and a director, and we're going to shoot a commercial better suited to the type of business I hope to be running; otherwise, I'll just be bootstrapping Mad for Mod indefinitely. What I have can run before the preview reel at the local movie house and even on local television channels and YouTube. Unfortunately, I'm not a natural."

"Impossible. You look like one of the most famous actresses of all time. Just pretend you're her."

One of the joys of meeting Paulie and Paolo was discovering that they loved Doris Day movies as much as I did. Well, almost. I shared a birthday with the actress, and my family had made it a tradition to watch one of her movies on every birthday of my life until they died in a car accident. Since then, Doris Day movies made me feel less lonely, and a literal lifetime of committing them to memory became the basis of my business. I'd met women who had become decorators after seeing *Pillow Talk* in 1959, but most had done it on the side while raising their families.

But tonight, the comparison to Doris Day didn't help. "That's the problem," I said. "I don't want to look like I'm trying to be someone I'm not. The goal is authenticity. I just want to be myself. I was fine when I winged it, but now I'm expected to write a script, and I trip over the words as soon as the camera turns on. I've spent my life being myself. I thought this would be the most natural thing in the world, but it turns out it's the most challenging."

The men looked at each other again and then at me. "This is a simple solution," Paolo said. "I will leave you two to work out the details while I return to bed. The bakery, she waits for no man." Paolo stood up, kissed Paulie on the top of his head, and left.

"This simple solution," I prompted. "Does it involve a stand-in double?"

"It involves an acting coach. Someone tasked with one job: making your acting authentic and believable."

"Isn't that the director's job?" I considered the numerous tasks in both Denton and Jules's job description and saw that my inability to deliver lines had been a bigger burden on them than I'd originally thought.

"The director oversees many things, but the better prepared you are for your role as star, the easier the task of making you look good is for him. You need someone on your team, and I know who you should hire."

"Who?"

"Me." He sat up straighter. "I've spent the past fourteen years as an acting coach. I collaborate one-on-one with clients and give them advice and mentoring to improve their performances. Three have gone from community theater to supporting roles in Hollywood movies. Plus, you know me, and you're comfortable around me. I've seen you at your most authentic, so I know what it is we want to capture when the camera is on."

My instinct was to say no, but this wasn't a bad suggestion. The problem with Paulie's offer was complicated: I knew of the dangers involved in being on the set where a murder had taken place, but by saying no, I'd insult my client. I remembered something I'd heard somewhere, probably the director's commentary of a movie on TCM.

"I should check with the director before making a decision. Ultimately my decision."

"Who's your director?"

"Jules Staton."

Paulie leaned back and slapped his knee. "That's fantastic! Jules and I went through the same theater program at the University of Texas. I'm sure she'll say yes. You have her number, right? Let's call her now."

There were at least five reasons why that was a bad idea. "You and Jules are friends?"

He shrugged. "We lost touch after graduation. Our class has a directory in the alumni section of the university website. If you're uncomfortable bringing it up tonight, I can come with you to the set and talk to her about it in person on Monday."

There were too many things riding on my response to decide this on my own. "Let me talk to her. I love the idea, but she's new to this project, and I'd rather not blindside her. Worst-case scenario, you can coach me in my spare time."

Paulie's energy had shifted, and for the first time since arguing with him over the orchid bathtub, I felt like I was talking to a stranger. "Sure, whatever you decide," he said. He pushed out his chair and stood. "I'll go find Rocky so you can be on your way."

ELEVEN

My cool departure from the Mangieri house was the opposite of the warm reception I'd received when I arrived. Not only had Paulie become aloof, but he'd returned my concept boards to the folio and handed it back to me as if it were a rejection of my design. I didn't just need their job, I wanted it. Mid-century modern enthusiasts were a small subset of the Dallas population, but they were passionate, appreciative, and loyal. Every one of my former clients felt like a friend, and this turn of events ushered in the possibility that my desire to expand might have negative repercussions on my old status quo.

I drove home with Rocky asleep in the passenger seat. His day had been almost as full as mine. I pulled alongside my hedges behind an unfamiliar pickup truck with wooden rails. Rocky padded along beside me and yanked his leash forward as I stopped to look in the back of the truck and discovered a few errant tomatoes.

Rocky and I went to the side door and entered the house. Tex had changed out of his suit and wore a black T-shirt, jeans, and an apron with a map of Texas. He stood in front of the stove, stirring the contents of a 16-quart stockpot. Similar pots sat on the other burners, and more filled the bin of my sink. Large collections of pots and pans were a staple of the modern woman's mid-century kitchen, and even though I'd been rebuilding my inventory from scratch, I'd already amassed enough to outfit a mess hall. Tex appeared to have put them to good use; the entire house smelled like marinara.

I unclipped Rocky's leash, and he jogged into the living room. "Why?" I asked.

"I thought you could use a home-cooked meal."

"I'm not talking about the fact that you're cooking to feed a small army, though I reserve the right to circle back to that if the mood strikes me. I'm talking about the complications that come when you least expect them."

Tex grabbed a clean plate, Eva Zeisel Harlequin, one of my favorite patterns from HallCraft, and filled it with rigatoni and then covered it with a generous ladle of red sauce. He carried the plate to the table and set it down and then filled two goblets with red wine and added them to the table, one in front of me and one before the chair to my left. I pulled a stainless steel fork with a small starburst pattern on the stem from the utensil drawer and sat while Tex opened the oven and used tongs to pull out a thick slice of garlic bread, which he rested on the edge of my plate. The bread rolled against the marinara. I picked the slice up and licked off the sauce before dropping it back on my plate when it burned my fingertips.

"Mmmmmmm." I speared three rigatoni and popped them into my mouth. *"Mmmmmmm,"* I said again with more emphasis. I chewed and swallowed then said, "Forget police work. You should start a restaurant."

Tex returned to the stove. He put the lid on the stockpot and turned down the heat then switched off the oven and came over to sit with me. He snagged the garlic toast from my plate and dunked it into the mess of sauce on my rigatoni, took a bite, and then redunked it and held it out for me. I leaned forward and bit into the crunchy slice. He wiped sauce from my lower lip with his thumb and popped his thumb into his mouth. "My grandmother's recipe. The best red sauce you'll ever have, and it has four ingredients."

I ate half of the portion on my plate before stopping to talk. The sauce was tangy and fragrant and the pasta rigid enough to hold onto the sauce. I didn't even care that I'd reek of garlic by the time I finished. It was divine.

"Why the sauce?" I finally asked. "I thought you were knee-deep in fish."

"I like to diversify." He grinned.

Tex and I had slipped into a synergistic relationship, but occasionally, he acted out of character and set off warning bells. I was hungry enough to ladle his sauce into a bowl and eat it like soup, but he was overdoing it on the thoughtful boyfriend routine. Tex had as much on his figurative plate as I had on mine. There was something else on his agenda. Historically, when I reached this level of insight, I called him out on what he was doing, but as long as I was installing a pool in secret, I decided to play along.

Besides, it *was* really good sauce.

"Where'd you get the tomatoes? They're not supposed to be in season for another couple of months."

"Clark has a tomato patch. After his high blood pressure diagnosis, he converted his backyard to a hothouse and started growing his own vegetables."

"Convenient," I said. "I didn't realize Clark was back at the Lakewood Police Department."

Officer Clark was one of several policemen I'd met over the course of my interactions with Tex. He'd been Nasty's partner when she was on the force and had the distinct honor of being the officer assigned to question me during the night I'd spent in jail. Despite all of the above, I thought of him fondly.

"Clark flexes between precincts. None of us can find officers to hire full-time. The part-timers make better pay and call the shots on their hours. And now we're competing with every other business in Dallas that's trying to hire. That's why I've been hitting the recruiting trips hard."

It reminded me of what Jimmy had said when I first called about the pool. Good work was hard to find no matter what your industry.

"That reminds me," I said. "I'm having a concrete floor poured in the garage while you're gone."

"Finally got tired of the dirt?"

"I've been thinking about using the garage for storage, but Thelma Johnson never had the floor sealed. I don't think it's wise to store inventory on a dirt floor."

Tex grinned. "You're lucky you work for yourself. Get things done on your schedule without worrying about employees and open jobs. You won't be lured by the offers of signing bonuses and extra weeks of vacation."

"Vay-kay-shun?" I sounded the word out as if it were as unfamiliar to me phonetically as in concept. "What's that?"

Tex leaned back in his chair and took a sip of his beer. "You'll get there. In the meantime, let's talk about Monday. We settled on a private security company to monitor surveillance from a remote location and we'll have people on-site. You'll have a private coach on the set."

"About that. I just came from the Mangieri house, and it turns out Paulie is an acting coach. We were talking about my dilemma, and he offered to help. I don't want to—"

"That's good. His being there will put you at ease and makes my undercover team look less obvious. You told him yes, right?"

"I told him I'd check with the director and see. I wanted to talk to you first. Should we put a civilian at risk like this?"

Tex, who'd been calmly discussing the shortage of police officers and the need to hire an outside security firm, now looked offended. "If you don't want to do this, I'll call it off."

"I didn't say I wasn't going to do it. But there are dangers here, and asking someone to be on that set is asking them to put themselves at risk. Paulie is the father of two young children. They need him."

Tex's expression changed from offense to hurt. "Do you think I'd ask you to do this if it weren't completely safe?" he asked. "Your clients are probably fantastic people, but I'm selfish. There's one person I care about more than anybody else, and that's you. You've been in more dangerous places thanks to your own decisions than the one I'm asking you to be at tomorrow, but if you want out, I'll come up with another plan."

Tex was right. Repeatedly, my choices had led me to life-threatening situations. He'd warned me off and then accepted that our minds worked similarly when it came to solving a puzzle, and homicides were puzzles. It was a new position, having him arrange what was ultimately a guardian angel for me, and going through with the commercial would solve any number of additional problems in my life.

"How am I supposed to explain why I have two coaches?"

"Everybody there saw your rough takes. I don't think that's going to be a question."

I sighed. "Fine, I'm in," I said. "Let me call Paulie and tell him before it gets too late."

AFTER DINNER, I'd worried about how to get him out of my house so I could have Jimmy come over and take measurements. A late meeting with the police commissioner solved that problem. Right after Tex drove away, I called Jimmy's Pools to get the ball rolling. He agreed to swing by and I unlocked the garage. By the time I went to bed, Jimmy had taken all the measurements he needed.

Saturday morning, after confirming Tex was on the road, I called Jimmy's Pools of Dallas and told them the coast was clear. A team of men arrived with a dig sheet, a large black tarp that indicated the size of the pool and the area they needed to dig up. Jimmy proudly drove a Bobcat excavator into the garage and broke ground.

Sunday passed in a blur of neglected housework and laundry. I occasionally turned toward the mirror and pretended I was being filmed, but each time, I felt self-conscious and wooden. By the end of the day, I was no closer to being camera-ready, but my baseboards sparkled like a dream.

Monday morning, I took Rocky for a walk around the block and then gave him the run of the house while I went to the Gaston Swim Club. I got in a solid forty-five-minute set then showered and dressed in a yellow pullover and matching capri pants from the estate of Gloria, the Braniff hostess. I knotted a yellow, green, and white floral scarf around my neck and laced up my white leather Keds, then fluffed my wet hair, slicked on pink lipstick, and headed to the film shoot. I pulled into the furniture store parking lot at seven forty-seven and entered the building ten minutes before eight.

Paulie was at the back of the store, talking to Jules. I waved to them and carried my wardrobe and train case into the powder room, where someone had taped a sheet of paper that said MADISON NIGHT CHANGING ROOM. I unzipped my garment bag and hung my different wardrobe options on the outside of the bathroom stall door. The door opened, and a voluptuous platinum blonde in a fitted shirt, tight pencil skirt, and red patent-leather pumps came out.

I recognized her immediately. It was Virginia, the exotic

dancer-turned Jumbos club owner. Right after recognition clicked into place, the reason she was there came with it.

"Virginia, what are you doing here?" I asked nervously.

"Captain Allen didn't tell you?" She smiled. "I'm going to teach you everything you need to know about getting comfortable in front of the camera."

TWELVE

I'D MET VIRGINIA NOT LONG AGO. SHE HAD STOOD IN AS TEX'S date on a recent undercover assignment, and that night, I'd learned that businesswomen come in all shapes and sizes. I couldn't erase Tex's bachelor past, and when you got down to it, I liked Virginia. She had a keen mind, specific talents, and sought out business opportunities just like me.

Well, maybe not just like me.

Virginia was as good a choice as any for my stand-in coach, and I appreciated the familiar face. "It's nice to see you again," I said.

"It's nice to see you too, darlin'." She turned away and eased the door to the powder room open, peeked out, and then stepped back and let it fall closed. "Captain Allen told me what's goin' on, and I'm happy to help. I knew Olivia from my days at the club. Word of her murder spread to us, and until the police know what happened to her, all my girls are scared."

"You think—hold on." I opened the door myself, peeked out to my left and right to confirm no one was in earshot, and closed the door again. There was a lock on the inside, and I turned it to deter interruption. "You think this might have been someone Olivia knew from Jumbos?"

"I don't know the details from the six months when I went freelance, but Jumbos' clientele is ninety percent cops. Dancing there is the safest place a girl could perform." Interesting observation. "But Olivia wasn't the only dancer who took jobs on the side."

"Jobs," I repeated. "Like bachelor parties?"

"No, honey, not like bachelor parties." She indulged me with a smile. "I don't know how Olivia got hired for this commercial, but it might not have had anything to do with a talent for acting."

I thought back to Arlene Fraleigh's response to seeing Olivia in the rough cut and wondered again at the commissioner's wife's shift in mood that night. She'd gone from loving and doting wife to laying down the law. I'd been so flustered by the limelight I'd been thrust into that I hadn't stopped to question if there was more behind Arlene's request than met the eye.

I didn't have time to question it now, either. As soon as Virginia mentioned the commercial, I felt nerves all the way to my fingertips. No matter what else was going on at the furniture store today, I was there to film a testimonial for the police. This commercial, in conjunction with the ones I was filming for Mad for Mod, would help expand Mad for Mod from being a small, word-of-mouth operation to one with city-wide presence. With a second mortgage on the property

next to my house, the expenses related to the pool installation, and more than half of my bank-secured loan spent on
Effie's salary and inventory acquisition, I needed an influx of
clients. Favor for Tex notwithstanding, I needed to do this,
and I needed all the help I could get.

"There's a man talking to the director," I told Virginia.
"His name is Paulie Mangieri, and he's here as my acting
coach. He knows nothing other than the fact that I'm a
novice in front of the camera. He might not like it when he
finds out you're here to do pretty much the same thing."

"Say no more. You wait here. I'll go use my considerable
charms on him so he'll want me to stay."

"He's gay," I said.

"Doesn't matter, darlin'. Men are men." She boosted two
of her considerable charms with her hands, unlocked the
bathroom door, and left. Almost immediately, she popped
her head back in. "Loosen up with hip rolls and then change
into this." She handed me a milky-white garment bag on a
hanger. "I'll go tell the director you're almost ready."

I unzipped the garment bag Virginia left for me and
stared at a short blue satin nightgown with a plunging neck-
line. There was no way I was filming a commercial for the
police dressed like that!

I dug into the back of my garment bag and found a light-
blue, floor-length chiffon dressing gown printed with
daisies, and a sheer pink duster. The dressing gown had a
white collar trimmed with a small ruffle and matching tiny
buttons down the placket. It had belonged to Robyn
Konopka, the administrative assistant for a duo of architects
from McKinney. Her estate included a carton of faded

ledgers that tracked their credits and debits, drafting pencils, protractors, and seven cartons of still-sealed jars of Nescafé 37 blend instant coffee.

I changed out of my yellow outfit and into the dressing gown, buttoned it to the collar, and attempted to tie the bow three times before it sat properly. There was a tentative knock on the powder room door, followed by a male voice. "Madison? It's Paulie. I'm here with hair and makeup. Can we come in?"

I opened the door. Paulie stood next to Aliyah, the makeup artist who'd been at the airplane hangar on my failed day of shooting. Today, she wore her long black braids pinned at her crown and knotted in the back.

Since my dressing room was also a ladies' room, I stepped out and let the door close behind me.

"Surprise," Aliyah said. She smiled. "I'm back!" She hugged me unexpectedly.

"That's great," I said. "Do you two know each other?"

"We just met." Aliyah glanced at Paulie. "I know he wants to rehearse your lines while Jules is blocking the scene, but I thought if we got you ready to shoot, you'd get more comfortable with your character."

"I am my character," I said. "I'm playing myself."

Paulie spoke up. "You're playing Madison Night, the best mid-century modern interior decorator in the Dallas–Fort Worth area. You're playing Madison Night, a woman who has a passion for mid-century design and wants to bring that passion into living rooms all over the city. You're playing Madison Night, business owner, dog owner, Doris Day fan."

"We're starting with the police commercial first," I told Paulie. "None of that matters."

"You're right. Let me work on your story while Aliyah gets you camera-ready."

He turned away and sat in the plastic-covered armchair on the end of the row. Just looking at the inventory, untouched by the ravages of time, made me forget all about my nerves. Arlene had said the place had been sitting abandoned for over a decade, and I saw no reason I shouldn't call her to thank her for the filming location—or perhaps even surprise her in person when the commercial wrapped.

Aliyah and I went back to the ladies' room. On the way, she picked up a folding chair, a flat piece of board, and a black nylon tote bag and carried them all inside.

"Paulie told me he's not just your coach, he's your client," Aliyah said.

I should have warned Paulie about what personal information he shared with the staff, but there was no way to warn him without letting him know what was going on. I remembered what Tex had said about surveillance and looked up at the corner of the room for a camera.

"What are you looking for?"

"This is a store. Do they have security cameras?"

"You can't put surveillance cameras in a bathroom. It's an invasion of privacy."

Aliyah unfolded a portable chair and told me to sit. She put the board over the sink and unpacked her tote, spreading out makeup and brushes, and then dabbed colors and powders onto my cheeks, eyes, and lips. I protested and said we were going with a natural look, and she told me not to worry.

"I'm glad you're back on the set," I said. "Who called you?"

"Bruce," she said. "We worked together on a couple of jobs around town, and he got me the original job with Denton."

"At the airplane hangar, you said Olivia replaced you with her hair and makeup team. What happened to her is awful, but I'm happy to have a familiar face here."

"Olivia had it coming," Aliyah said in such a matter-of-fact way that I questioned whether Aliyah knew what had happened. She picked up a curling wand and wrapped a section of my hair around the barrel. "Olivia used friends who could help her and threw them away when she was done. I could name ten people who wanted her out of the picture. Some would put me on that list too. I guess I'm lucky she had me fired so I have an alibi for her murder."

It was an unusually callous thing to say, and I stiffened. Aliyah was working on my hair, and she bent down and glanced at my face. "Are you cold?"

"Yes," I said. "I should have brought a space heater."

"Wait here. Bruce set up a few by the film set. I'll get one." She set the curling iron down and left me alone.

If I'd temporarily forgotten why the commercial was moving forward, Aliyah's callous comments brough reality back. With the exception of the people I recognized as Tex's undercover plants, everybody here was a suspect.

I hopped up from my seat and peeked inside Aliyah's black tote. I didn't know what I was looking for, but it seemed convenient for her to carry her own supplies, and if she carried something threatening, I wanted to know. I stuck my hand between cans of hairspray and mousse and pushed them to the side, angling the bag toward the window for light. Something small and pale pink glittered at the bottom of the bag. I reached in and pulled out the object.

It was a shiny fingernail with a sparkling diamond in the center, just like the one missing from Olivia's left hand the day I'd found her body.

THIRTEEN

I HELD THE FINGERNAIL BETWEEN MY THUMB AND INDEX FINGER and examined it closely. On the underside of it, I could see a rough texture where the nail glue must have adhered it to Olivia's natural fingernail. A divot was missing from the base of the nail. Overall, I'd say it hadn't been removed on purpose.

Everything about the fingernail told me it was a clue. I looked back at Aliyah's black bag. If I put the fingernail back, Aliyah might find it and throw it out or worse, melt it down and destroy it for good. If I took it, then there would be nothing linking the makeup artist to the murdered dancer-turned-actress. I had to decide quickly because a whole crew of people waited for me out front, and Aliyah could return at any given moment.

While I stood frozen in indecision, the last stall of the bathroom opened. Nasty came out. She wore a charcoal-gray, fitted pantsuit with a white shirt open at the collar and red-patent leather heels. I labeled her Wall Street Barbie in my head but suspected saying it aloud might undo the great inroads we'd made toward friendship.

"Put the fingernail back in the bag," Nasty instructed. She pointed to the small glittering object pinched between my fingertips.

"What are you doing here?" I looked at the stall behind her. "Have you been hiding in there all this time?"

"Tex told you he hired private security. I own the most successful private security company in Dallas. Are you going to tell me you didn't put two and two together?"

"I've been preoccupied."

"Listen to me. Put the fingernail back in the bag. I know you think it's the clue that's going to lead to a conviction, but you're jumping to conclusions. Aliyah might be the one who put those nails on Olivia at a previous job, or she might have seen them on Olivia and gotten a set for herself. She could have borrowed that gig bag from another makeup artist. Temporary nails are available at every salon in the area. You don't know enough about what you just found to know what it means."

Reluctantly, I tossed the nail back into the bag. Now that one dilemma was behind me, I explored another. "This is supposed to be a closed set. How are you going to explain your presence?"

"I'm your publicist." She handed me a business card for a PR firm called Nasty Business. "Nobody talks to you without me knowing. You don't agree to anything, and you always, always stay in my line of vision."

I didn't love knowing Nasty was on the set, but that had

more to do with my lack of confidence in my acting abilities. Nasty made me a better version of myself, but that didn't mean I wanted her to see me fail.

I fanned myself with her card. "You heard what Aliyah just said about Olivia, right? Don't you think that was suspicious?"

"Yes," she said, and then added as an afterthought, "Let me be the one to tell Tex about the fingernail."

I leaned back against the outside of the bathroom stall. I was facing the small mirror over the sink, and from my reflection, I could tell the idea didn't sit well with me. The garish makeup left my features exaggerated, and I looked troubled.

"I'm not about to start keeping secrets from Tex. That's not how we work."

"I'm not asking you to lie. I just—" She cleared her throat. "I don't think Tex has a suspect, but the makeup woman wasn't even on his radar. He went to considerable efforts to ensure that the film set is safe for everybody there, but don't think for a second he won't shut it down if he thinks this plan is too dangerous."

"What do you want?" There was a beat of silence. "Let's not do this dance. Tell me how you want to play this."

"You want to film your commercial. Tex wants to catch the killer. I want to earn the considerable fee the city is paying me so they'll hire me again. Let's make it through the shoot, and I'll come over to your house tonight and tell Tex then. You can repot daisies while you eavesdrop if it makes you feel better."

Nasty had a way of throwing in zingers when I least

expected them. She would never understand my passion for mid-century modern design or what Doris Day movies meant to me, but I was starting to wonder if for all Nasty had, she lacked passion. Her life was go, go, go toward success, success, success. She'd left the police force as a patrol officer and started Big Bro Security, a privatized security company that, in five years, contracted out to the most respected businesses in the area. She had a one-year-old baby with one of Dallas's wealthiest men, a seventy-something with a youthful attitude, a healthy heart, and a prescription for little blue pills. She'd repeatedly turned down his marriage proposals, citing her freedom as more important than his cash. Nasty was like no other woman I'd ever met. It figured we'd end up here.

I gave her an ultimatum. "If you don't come over and tell Tex tonight—in front of me—then I'm not only going to tell him, but I'll also let him know you said not to."

"What is this, the fourth grade? This is a murder investigation, Madison. I'm not going to hide your note from the boy you like so he'll ask me out instead."

I didn't know what kind of elementary school Nasty attended, but the only thing I'd worried about in fourth grade had been softball. Boys hadn't entered the picture until junior high.

"Fine," I said. "Now what?"

"Now you take your time getting ready while I poke around the set." She left.

Nasty was right. I didn't know what the fingernail meant. But I wasn't itching to spend more time with Aliyah in close quarters, so I picked up the curling iron and worked through the rest of my hair in the same manner she'd started. When the door eased open, I was finishing the last section. Aliyah entered, holding a small gray space heater. She plugged it in and turned it on, and a gentle warmth blossomed into the room.

"You're going to put me out of a job," Aliyah said.

"I'm used to doing things myself."

"Don't tell the director that," she said. "I need this gig." She stood behind me and fluffed my barrel curls with her fingers.

I wasn't the type to spend hours on my hair, but I couldn't deny that it looked good. Of course, the entire effect would be gone the moment I dove into the pool to swim laps tomorrow. Hair and makeup were unimportant efforts, as far as I was concerned.

"Done," she said. "Your coaches are waiting for you outside, but you should check in with Jules before you head off to rehearse."

"Are you coming with me?"

"No, I'm going to clean up in here and make sure I didn't lose anything. I'm notorious for leaving something behind on a set."

I felt a shiver through my body despite the space heater. "Nerves," I explained.

I left the powder room and scanned the interior of the store. Jules had finished rearranging the furniture in the back, and a man I hadn't seen before adjusted a giant light that aimed at the impromptu set. Paulie and Virginia sat together, watching him. Two young production assistants, one male and one female, fluttered around the set.

Bruce, the beefy tattooed man, instructed members of his crew to secure a large white bounce screen to the top of a metal frame that defined our film set. He aimed key lights at the grouping of furniture in the background then adjusted a portable white wall so the light bounced off it. It was a little like watching a choreographed number at the ballet but with more sweat and denim.

I walked toward Paulie and Virginia. Their heads were together, and they looked like coconspirators. As I walked, my pink duster billowed out behind me. Virginia scanned my dressing gown, and her forehead wrinkled.

"Before you say anything, I'm not wearing a revealing nightgown to film a testimonial about the police," I said before she could protest my choice. "I'm not sure why I should wear a nightgown, but this is more appropriate."

"Who told you to wear a nightgown? I gave you my best cocktail dress."

Paulie stood. "Madison, you are perfection personified." He sent a quick scolding glance at Virginia. "Do you want to run lines?"

"I haven't seen a script," I admitted. "I'd like a chance to read it over before we start so I can put it into my own words."

Jules joined us. She held a sheet of paper. "Madison," she interrupted. "Let's get a walk-through so the crew can check the lighting and I can see what we're working with." She turned away.

I followed her. A stack of cue cards sat against the wall. The memory of not being able to read from them the other day came back to me, as did my nerves.

"I'd love to look over the script first if that's okay with you."

"Just wing it. You'll have time to work your script out during lunch." She stood behind a flatscreen tablet mounted to a C-stand.

The male PA jumped in front of me with a black-and-white clapboard I'd learned was called a slate. "Lakewood Police PSA Test. Nightgown Take One."

"Hello, I'm Madison Night," I said.

Jules looked out from behind the monitor. "I haven't called 'Action' yet."

"Oh. Sorry." I fussed with the bow on my nightgown.

The PA jumped in front of me. "Lakewood Police PSA Test. Nightgown Take Two." He clapped the slate again.

Jules counted down, "Five, four, three," and then held her fingers up in a peace sign, and then just her index finger, and then pointed at me. I waited for her to say "Action." Instead, after an awkward pause, she said, "Cut. What now, Madison?"

"I was waiting for you to say 'Action.'"

"I thought you did this before."

"I filmed my first commercial on my phone."

"Okay." She turned to the crew and then back to me. "One of the PAs will announce the take. I'll count you down. When I point at you, you go. Got it?"

"Got it."

Jules nodded at the PA. He updated the slate and then said, "Lakewood Police PSA Test. Nightgown Take three." Clap.

Jules counted down five-four-three, then peace sign, then point.

I cleared my throat. "Hello, I'm Madison Night. I'm a resident of the Lakewood/White Rock Lake community, and I just want to say thank you to our police force." Well, that sounded lame. I stood in Jules's mock living room configuration and placed my hand on the back of a leather chair. I squeezed the leather to give my nervous energy a release. "I don't like that. Can I start over?"

Jules kept her eyes on the monitor. "Just keep talking, Madison. It doesn't matter what you say. We're checking audio, lighting levels, and adjusting the set."

"Oh. Right."

"Start over." She looked into her viewfinder and said, "We're still rolling."

"Hello, I'm Madison. I'm a fan of the local police department, and I'd like to tell you why." I glanced away from the camera to Virginia and Paulie. Paulie stood. He turned his back on me and walked away with his phone pressed to his head. I looked around for Nasty, but she was on her phone too. I went blank on what to say. The unfamiliar man I'd noticed earlier slid a green filter over a large light. It was Officer Clark. Tex had said I'd see familiar faces, but the surprise gave me a jolt.

Clark held my stare, and I knew I had to say something. "I spent the night in prison once," and then added, "I wasn't supposed to be in prison. It was a mix-up, and a different police department put me there. The Lakewood Police Department never would have done that." I smiled broadly. I pushed my hands into the pockets on my duster. "I can't tell you what it means to go to bed at night knowing I've got the police with me."

Snickers broke out around me, and even Virginia's eyes widened. "Oh! I don't mean that! I mean how they protect and serve."

Jules called, "Cut."

I glanced at Bruce, who held a bar with a microphone dangling from the end over my head. "Don't you get tired holding that?"

He adjusted his grip, and the wand dropped lower. The tip of the microphone bonked me on the head. I stepped out from under it and rubbed the spot where it hit. Jules turned her head and called out, "We need hair and make-up!" She turned back to me. "Madison, try not to touch your hair."

It was a good thing Tex had his own undercover operatives on the set, because it was nearly impossible to keep track of everyone there. I endured a forty-five minute wait while the crew adjusted lights, shifted chair placement, and repositioned sound-absorbing barriers. Aliyah touched up my lipstick fourteen times, and I was desperate to satisfy an itch on the crown of my head that I'd been instructed not to touch. The promise of lunch kept everyone focused while I kept trying to work out what I wanted to say. It was a nightmare.

"Let's go through it one more time. Madison, use the cue cards this time. They were written for Olivia, so we made some adjustments, but I want to see how this compares to your earlier efforts." Jules pointed to the PA, who picked up the stack of forgotten cue cards and knelt in front of Jules, holding one up. "Just read through them even if they don't fit your story."

"Okay." I smoothed down my duster and licked my lips. "Okay."

"Lakewood Police PSA Test. Nightgown Take seventeen." Clap.

I folded my hands in front of me and read from the first cue card. "Hello, my name is Olivia Jean, and I've been a bad girl. I need to be punished." I looked up from the cue cards at Jules, who spun her hand in a circle, encouraging me to keep reading. "I'm on the verge of my big break, and it's because of police commissioner Fraleigh." This didn't feel right. There was no reason to mention the commissioner, especially in a public service announcement about the police. But I hadn't flubbed my reading yet, so I kept going. "Commissioner Fraleigh—remember that name—coached me in *private* and taught me everything I need to succeed in Hollywood by using my God-given talents. If anything happens to me, Police Commissioner Edward Fraleigh is the person responsible."

FOURTEEN

NOBODY ON THE SET MOVED. I STOOD STILL, UNSURE HOW TO follow up what sounded like Olivia's from-the-grave implication of Police Commissioner Fraleigh in her murder. I glanced side to side without moving my head, trying to gauge the reaction of the crew. They watched Jules. She held up her hand and then closed it into a fist. "Cut," she said. She leaned back from the camera. "Let's break for lunch."

I stared at her. How could she act like that was normal? I'd just read, in a dead woman's words, an accusation of the police commissioner. The same police commissioner who'd arranged for all of us to stand here filming. Was that how a film set worked? Were we all going to pretend we hadn't heard what we'd heard because we wanted to keep our jobs?

The crew immediately dropped what they were doing and went to the front of the store, where caterers had set up a spread of food. Paulie lingered nearby. I stepped over cables to reach the front row of chairs where he stood.

"We have a problem," he said. "When I offered to coach you, I didn't realize where you were. I thought I could help you, but this might be too far."

"I'll get better," I said. "I didn't know I was supposed to write a script. I wasn't prepared, but I've never seen those cue cards before today."

He looked at me in confusion, deep creases that made an eleven between his eyebrows. I considered how best to manage this, him being not just my acting coach but also a client. Finally, understanding dawned on his face, and he reached out and grabbed my hands, his eyes wide.

"Madison! I'm not insulting you. I have a scheduling conflict!" He held up his cell phone as if it were evidence. "Paolo called. Maggie got into a mess at school today. Something about a mudball fight. He can't leave the bakery, and it's not the sort of thing you ask your neighbors to handle for you."

The nervous tension in my neck and shoulders eased away, and everything shifted. "Of course, you have to attend to Maggie." I took my spare hand and patted it on top of his hand on my forearm. "I'll be fine. This—that—what you just saw, that was a dry run."

Paulie thanked me for understanding and left. I watched him go past the crew at the catering table and say something to Jules. They hugged briefly, and then he left. Relief at one less person to worry about seeped into my body. The bright sunlight cast a glare over the windows, and I lost sight of him.

Virginia approached me with a thin black robe. "Darlin', if you're going to eat, you better put this on."

I took it from her and put it on over my dressing gown. Fluffy layers of chiffon were smushed underneath, but at least I didn't have to add food stains to my rapidly growing list of concerns.

"Come on, let's get some lunch," she said.

"I'm not hungry."

"Don't punish yourself because you got a line wrong. It's a read-through, and that isn't even your script. You probably just need to eat."

"But I didn't get a line wrong. Not on that last take, at least. I read what was written on the cue card."

"It's okay, Madison. Nobody's perfect their first time." She hooked her hand into the crook of my elbow and steered me away from the filming set. Like everyone else, she acted as if I'd been the one to make a mistake, but I couldn't help wondering if Edward Fraleigh was more involved with Olivia than he'd let on.

AFTER LUNCH, we returned to the set. The cue cards sagged against the wall. Aliyah touched up my lipstick and smoothed my hair, and Bruce turned on enough lights to illuminate a baseball stadium at midnight. Jules came over to where I stood. "We're going to try the cue cards again."

I looked at the sagging stack. "Can I review them first?"

"Not those. This time, I wrote a script for you." She put her hands up in front of her as if expecting a tantrum. "Your publicist approved it."

I looked over my shoulder at Nasty. She caught my eye and responded with a shrug.

"I'm sure it's fine," I said.

Jules continued as if I hadn't said a word. "Let's get a couple takes so I have something to edit tonight. If you mess something up, start over at the beginning of the sentence. After we get this, we'll move on to your commercial. Got it?"

"Got it," I repeated.

She waved the female PA over to hold the cue cards. The young woman took the stack of whiteboards from Jules and flipped through them. I assumed she was looking for tricky pronunciations or other word bombs. She nodded and then followed Jules. She squatted on the floor with the first cue card aimed my way.

"Lakewood Police PSA Test. Nightgown Take eighteen." Clap.

Jules counted me down and pointed. "Hello, I'm Nadison Might." I caught myself. "I'm Madison Night." I cut my eyes to the crew. A few snickered. I wanted to quit already, but I had to keep going. "I'm a local decorator. Last year, someone vandalized my studio." I glanced up from the cards to Jules but then remembered why we were here and kept going. "If not for the quick response from the Lakewood Police Department, I might not be here to tell you about it."

My nerves faded as I remembered that day and many others when Tex had responded to help me out. This was a true story, and it did exactly what I'd been tasked to do: it made the police look good by describing their swift and effective response. Virginia stood slightly behind Jules and pointed to her smile.

I smiled back and continued. "All over this town, residents count on the police to be there when they're needed. I'm here to tell you that you can count on the Lakewood Police Department." I read the last line on the card. "They've got your back."

Jules held her hand up and, three seconds later, made a fist. "Cut," she said.

This time, the response was audible. Crew sprang to action, repositioning lights and filters and microphones and sound tiles. It wasn't the best reading in the world, but I'd gotten through it, and that alone was a victory.

I changed into a yellow shirt-waist dress, and we went through the commercial three more times. Each time, I felt more natural. At this rate, we'd finish with everything today, which worked for me but might not be enough time for the investigation to uncover shady activity.

At three forty-five, Jules stopped for the day. "Can everybody come back for an eight o'clock call time tomorrow?"

"Wait," I said. "What about my commercial? Aren't we filming that too?" The energy in the store changed. Crew members glared at me. I misunderstood their anger. "Was I misinformed?"

"We're nowhere near wrapping on the police endorsement," Jules said. "I need to review what we got today before knowing how to proceed. Your commercial will come after that. There's no point paying the staff to show up if you can't be here tomorrow, so it's your call."

Bruce mumbled something to Clark, and others turned their backs on me and walked away. I hated losing another day of decorating work but reminded myself that I was getting something out of this too. "Tomorrow at eight works for me."

As the crew covered the equipment in plastic tarps, I walked over to the stack of original cue cards and flipped through them. When I got to the last one, I felt the color rising into my cheeks. Virginia was right; I was the one who'd flubbed the last line. *If anything happens for me, Police Commissioner Fraleigh is the person responsible.* That one word, "for" instead of "to," changed the meaning of the entire testimonial. Olivia had given the commissioner credit for her big break, not blamed him for her death. The humiliating part wasn't that I'd made the mistake but that I'd been so sure that I was right.

I left the cue cards in their stack and went to the powder room to collect my things. Aliyah's gig bag was gone and with it the lone clue I'd turned out after an entire day on set. I didn't bother to change out of my yellow dress. I left my garment bag hanging on the bathroom stall door, collected my handbag, and exited the powder room. Nasty held the front door open for me. The rest of the crew was in the parking lot, and Jules was alone, smoking a cigarette by her dirty Fiat.

As I got closer, I noticed how no one talked to Jules. She was the director, which put her in charge, but all day, I'd found her off by herself. No matter what she knew of me from Hudson, she'd done me a huge favor by writing a believable script for me.

I left Nasty and approached Jules. "Thank you for what you wrote," I said. "I didn't know you knew about my recent background, but that made all the difference."

She had her mirrored sunglasses on, and I couldn't see her eyes, but her expression seemed friendly and open. "I was curious about you, so I looked you up. That seemed like a good story to tell."

"I'm surprised you didn't use something that happened in the case you made a movie about," I said to bridge the gap between us. "It would have worked as a teaser for the film."

"Someone I care about was almost destroyed by the police during that case," she said. "I took this job because I could use the money, but I can't say I'm the Lakewood PD's biggest fan."

Before I could react, a woman from the catering company beckoned Jules to join her. She held the door so I could pass through, and then she went back inside.

I passed the crew and pasted a smile on my face for their benefit. "See you tomorrow," I said lightly. A few nodded at me, but none showed any outgoing friendliness.

I walked around the back of the store to where I'd parked my vintage blue Alfa Romeo and rested my handbag on the passenger seat. The catering woman came out the back door and carried two bulging bags of trash outside. She set them down and propped the door open with the torn sandbag I'd tripped over the first day I was here. She grabbed two more bags from inside and moved them out. I left my car and went over to help her. Cleaning up at the end of a day's work on a job site was a habit, and after a day of being told I couldn't lift, move, or help with anything, it felt good to do something.

"I'll get the last one," I said. I picked up the garbage bag and carried it to the dumpster. The woman took it from me and threw it on top of the first two. The bag broke on contact, and food scraps spilled out along with a folded white cue card.

"Did you throw that away?" I asked, pointing at the cue card.

"The cardboard? The woman in charge said it was trash. Why? You don't need it, do you?"

We both stared at the cardboard, now covered with streaks of avocado and coarse-ground brown mustard.

"I don't know if I need it or not," I said truthfully but for reasons other than what the caterer probably meant. I anchored my sneaker-clad foot on the side of the dumpster. I bent over the top, reached for the cue card, and hopped back down.

"You should have changed," the caterer said. "Your dress is smudged." She pointed to a smear of green avocado on the skirt of my yellow dress.

"I guess I know what I'll be doing tonight."

"Soak the fabric under icy water before you do anything," she said. "Rub in some liquid dishwashing detergent and then put it back in cold water for fifteen minutes and wash it in the hottest water you can."

"You know a lot about stain removal."

"I'm a caterer. It's a hazard of the trade."

I thanked the woman for her domestic advice. She went back to the rear entrance, moved the sandbag out of the way, and let the door close behind her. When I was sure I was alone, I unfolded the cue card. I immediately recognized the card that I'd read from before lunch.

If anything happens to me, Police Commissioner Edward Fraleigh is the person responsible.

It was as I'd read it. It was an accusation. Someone had pointed the finger at Edward Fraleigh.

I'd been right all along, but the thought was of little comfort now. I didn't know who was responsible for making me read that line in a room filled with people, but Jules had been the one to throw the card away. She hadn't reacted in the slightest to the information when I read it aloud, which might have been because she expected me to say it. And when I'd approached her about the cue cards, she expressed hostility toward the local police.

Now that I thought about it, I didn't know why Denton had been replaced by Jules, but considering these new facts, it seemed a worthwhile piece of information to obtain.

FIFTEEN

By the time I left, I had a laundry list of suspects that implicated Aliyah, Jules, and Police Commissioner Edward Fraleigh himself. Drew Billings had been the one to arrange for me to film the commercial at the store, but according to the message left with Effie, Billings no longer worked for the commissioner. And questions surrounded Denton's removal from the project. The only person I'd talked to today who didn't seem suspicious was the caterer.

Although...

No. I refused to believe someone that skilled in stain removal could be a murderer.

Although...

No. Absolutely not.

I'd give her contact information to Tex just in case.

I drove home, where Rocky waited for me inside the front door. I clipped on his leash and took him for a quick walk around the block, ending at the satellite office. Several packages were stacked by the front door. I was dirty enough that there was no point changing before moving them inside, so I unlocked the door then dragged the parcels into my workspace. I unclipped Rocky's leash, and he ran through the interior with the delight of a Shih Tzu.

The first time I entered this building, it had smelled of mildew. I asked my friends to help empty the place and scour it from ceiling to floor, and when all three of them turned me down, I enlisted a team of professionals. It took a quarter of the time it would have taken me to do it myself and eliminated the two-day window I would have needed for my body to recover.

Once the interior was clean and empty, I hired a concrete service to raise the sinking foundation with two jacks and pour a concrete floor for the inside. They thought I was kidding when I asked them to seal it with a bright-yellow epoxy. When we reached a stalemate, I gave them a tour of my kitchen, which tipped them to my side. The floor wasn't just my favorite part of the remodel, it had gotten me into their sales brochure.

I'd painted the dark paneling in a blend of Spun Sugar, a white shade with luminescent particles, and Lemon Twist, a bold yellow from the paint collection I'd endorsed for my local paint store. The mixture created a sweet yellow shade that sparkled in the sunlight. I refreshed the trim around the windows with Spun Sugar and replaced all hardware with vintage finds accumulated in my recent round of inventory acquisition. I'd had to pay extra to have one estate take the starburst escutcheon from their front door, but it looked sensational against the Lemon Twist front door.

When the packages were inside, I locked the door behind me and walked Rocky home. A silver Saab sat alongside the hedges behind Tex's Jeep. Nasty's promise to visit felt like it came days ago, not just this morning. I carried the soiled cue card inside and set it by the front door.

Nasty was sitting on the blue tweed sofa in my Mercury-mission, space-themed sitting room. Her blazer was draped over the arm of the sofa, and her red stilettos were cast off a few feet from where her son, Huxley, sat on the carpet. Huxley clutched a plush rocket in his fist and chewed on the landing gear. Rocky trotted over to Huxley and stuck his nose in the area of the boy's diaper.

"What happened to you?" Nasty asked me.

I looked down at my dress. The avocado smear had been joined by brown streaks of dirt from lugging the packages. I ignored her question and went with my more pressing one. "Did you see anything suspicious about the catering staff today?"

"No. Why?"

I held up my hand. "Where's Tex?"

"In your basement."

I looked over my shoulder toward the direction of the house where the storm cellar door was outside. I'd never once seen a mouse in or around the house. I turned back to Nasty. "Doing what?"

She shook her head. "I've learned not to ask about what goes on in this house."

"Can I leave Rocky with you for a few minutes? If I have a prayer of getting the stains out of this dress, I have to soak it now."

"Do what you have to do." She glanced at Rocky and Huxley and then went back to typing on her screen.

I changed out of my dress and into bright-green knit stirrup pants and a cotton green, pink, and white Fair Isle sweater. I carried my dress to the kitchen and submerged it in cold water. I added a tray of ice from the freezer to keep it cold and set a timer for ten minutes. From the window, I saw Tex climb out of the storm cellar. I knocked on the window and waved him in. He closed the storm cellar doors, slid a padlock into place, came around the side of the house, and joined me in the kitchen.

"Hey," he said. We kissed hello, and he slung his arms around me. "You hungry? There's a pecan pie in the fridge."

I ducked out from under his arms and opened the fridge. "You made a pecan pie?"

"Imogene made a pecan pie. Imogene made seven pecan pies, and she gave me one."

Imogene was the volunteer who helped around the police station. She was a mystery writer who relished the idea of spending her days conducting real-life research. After five months of her questioning every detail at the precinct, Tex presented her with a confidentiality contract he made up in his office. He had no intention of enforcing it, but things got a lot quieter after she signed.

"I'm hungry, and I'm tired, and I'm dirty. And Nasty is in my house."

"I heard that," she called out from two rooms away.

"Have you two talked yet?" I asked.

"She said she wanted to wait for you."

I was impressed. I'd only half expected Nasty to keep her

word. "Let's go." I led Tex to the Glenn Den. I sat on the sofa next to Nasty, and Tex sat in a plush armchair that I'd had recovered in space gray. Rocky, having tired of Huxley, curled up in his dog bed. Huxley pulled himself up to a standing position and stumbled two steps toward Tex then collapsed into a sitting position. He grabbed a fistful of Tex's jeans and tugged on them like a trucker honking his horn.

"Huxley, no," Nasty said.

Huxley stopped tugging on Tex's pants and looked at Nasty for further instruction. She closed her laptop and bent down, picking up his rocket and handing it to him. I held my breath, waiting for something maternal like "Leave Mommy's friend's pants alone" to come out of her mouth, but it was not to be.

"He's got about twenty minutes with that rocket until he decides Tex's pants are more exciting, so let's do this." She looked at me. "Did you tell him?"

"You told me not to," I said.

"You're keeping information about a case from me because Nasty asked you to?" Tex asked. The tension in his voice was unmistakable.

"No!"

Nasty held up her hands. "You've got a new suspect. Aliyah Rashad. Hair and makeup. Your victim was missing a fingernail, right?"

"Right."

"I found the fingernail inside Aliyah's makeup bag."

Tex turned to me. "Did you know about this?"

I looked at Nasty. She jumped in. "I told Madison to let me tell you because I thought you would shut down the commercial if you thought she was in danger. But if you shut things down, we lose all access to your suspects."

Tex did not look happy. "How much time do you spend with hair and makeup?" he asked me.

It wasn't worth lying. "Aliyah sticks as close to me as my shadow."

Nasty set her laptop aside and leaned forward with her elbows on her thighs. "If Aliyah was the murderer and she finds that fingernail in her bag, she's going to toss it, and you'll lose the evidence you have that links her to Olivia's murder. If she's not the murderer, she won't think twice about having a broken fingernail in her makeup bag, and it'll be there when you search her. So that one piece of evidence, if you obtain it, probably does more to prove her innocence than her guilt."

I had to give Nasty credit. She was usually a step ahead of everybody else in the room, and this was no different.

Tex nodded in agreement. "Did anything else suspicious happen?" Tex asked.

"Yes," I said.

"No," Nasty said at the same time.

"Which is it?" Tex asked. Nasty looked at me.

"The cue cards?" I reminded her.

"I checked the cue cards when you went to get lunch," she said. "You made a mistake when you read them."

I stood up, got the cue card that I'd retrieved from the dumpster, and handed it to Nasty. She unfolded it and read then looked up. "Where'd you get this?"

"The trash out back."

"When?"

"After you left."

Tex looked mad. "You were supposed to stick to her like glue," he said to Nasty.

"Can you not talk about me like I'm not here?" I asked. They turned their attention to me. "I am not without skills of my own," I added.

Tex and Nasty shifted their eyes from my face to the card. "Who wrote that?" Tex asked.

I shrugged. "Someone from the original set, I'd guess. The one at the airplane hangar. I still don't know why Olivia came to where we were filming at the furniture store. I thought the whole purpose of changing the filming location was to keep her from causing any problems after she was replaced."

Tex nodded at me. "Good observation. I'll find out who leaked that information." He pointed to the card. "What happened when you read it?"

"Nothing," I said. "As soon as the words were out of my mouth, I expected a response. But everybody acted as if I was the one who made the mistake. Jules called cut, and we broke for lunch. I tried to explain, but even Virginia believed I read the wrong word." I thought back to how I'd lingered behind while the rest of the crew went to the food table and had checked the stack of cue cards. "I waited until I was alone, and I looked at the cards. The last card in the stack was different than this one."

I set the card on the floor, and Huxley immediately shifted to all fours and crawled toward it. I picked it back up and propped it on the bottom shelf of the built-in bookcases behind the sofa.

"Where'd that one come from?" Tex asked, pointing at the card.

Nasty leaned against the back of the sofa and waited for my response.

"It was in the trash. I helped the caterer with the garbage, and one of the bags split open when she tossed it inside the bin. This was inside, buried under food scraps."

I expected one of the two of them to confirm that I'd just admitted to digging around in the garbage, but I forgot these two knew that was as common a habit as my morning cup of coffee.

Nasty asked, "You think the caterer is involved?"

"At this point, I wouldn't rule anyone out," I said honestly.

Tex turned to Nasty. "Ask around. See if you can find out who tossed it. If the caterer took it herself, that's incriminating enough to send one of the Sues to ask her some questions."

SIXTEEN

Nasty stood and stretched then bent down to pick up Huxley. He held his arms up and reached toward her. She lifted him and cradled his tush with the crook in her arm. He tucked one arm next to her side and hugged her with the other, his little hand closing around a fistful of her shirt. I wondered how many of the men in Nasty's life became transfixed at the idea that this small baby boy was the key to a possible wardrobe malfunction.

"I'll have something for you to go on before the call time tomorrow morning." She moved Huxley's fist from her shirt and closed her hand around it. He looked up at her in adoration. "Madison, can you walk me out?"

I glanced at Tex. He stared at the cue card. "Sure," I said. I stood and followed her, unsure of what she had to say that she didn't want Tex to hear.

She waited until the door to my house closed behind her and turned to face me. "You need to get it together on that set," she said. "If you can't deliver the lines, they're going to replace you with someone else."

"Maybe they should. Maybe Tex should assign someone from the police force to film the PSA instead."

"Tex can't spare anybody from the force. Until you entered the picture, Tex had one source for favors from women, and thanks to the police commissioner's wife, they're off-limits."

"There are other solutions."

"Sure, there are. But where do they leave you and your follow-up commercials?"

"I can't do this indefinitely. My business is booming. It should be my top priority. You of all people should understand that."

"I do. Your old commercial may have made you a local celebrity, but you're never going to get another opportunity to film a legit commercial with a crew like the one on the PSA. Don't lose sight of what you can get out of this too. It's not all about the police."

Nasty shifted Huxley to her other hip. She leaned back to counter his weight and then used her spare hand to sweep a strand of copper-highlighted hair away from her face. "Madison, did I ever tell you I acted in high school?"

"No," I said, my self-esteem worsening.

"That's because I didn't act in high school." She was silent for a moment. "I tried out, but I didn't get a role. Do you know why?"

"No. Why?"

"I suck at acting. I know who I am, and I don't like the idea of pretending to be someone else."

I stared at her, dumbfounded. For as long as I'd known her, Nasty had shown me that anything was possible if you put your mind to it. She conquered goal after goal with a drive I'd rarely seen in others, and just when it seemed as if she were sacrificing her personal life for success, she'd gotten pregnant and had Huxley. And here she was, telling me there was something she'd once wanted that she didn't get. And the ongoing revelation of Nasty was that she lacked any resentment over that life-defining moment in her past.

"You're like me that way," she continued. "You walk around in clothes from the sixties in a world of people in stretchy jeans and yoga pants, and you don't care that you don't fit in." She tipped her head to the side. "Stop trying to be Olivia. Stop trying to be an on-screen actor. Your original commercial was cheap, but it worked because you were authentic. Just be yourself."

"Thank you," I said.

"You're welcome. Now show up for your call time tomorrow and do your job. Leave the investigation to me and Tex."

She left. I stood outside until her taillights disappeared at the end of the street and then let myself back into my house. I wasn't sure what I would say if Tex asked me what she'd wanted to talk about. I was a little in shock by it all.

Turns out, I needn't have worried. Tex was in the kitchen with his keys in one hand and the cue card in the other.

"I'm going to take off," he said. "Fraleigh is breathing down my neck on this one. I've got a late meeting with the Sues, and there's no time to waste."

I pointed to the cue card. "Have you considered that

Commissioner Fraleigh could have been involved?" I rephrased the question. "Do you know who hired Olivia in the first place?"

"Yes and yes. And I can't say more than that. Thanks for your help today, Night. Nasty said you were good." He hooked his arm around my neck and kissed the top of my head and then left.

Something was going on. First Nasty confessed a failure to me, and then she told Tex I'd done well on today's shoot? And now Tex was rushing out of my house. I'd long since gotten beyond the jealous notion that they'd restarted the fling they'd had before I met either one of them, but something was swirling around under the surface, and I was the odd man out.

I hated being the odd man out.

I helped myself to a slice of Imogene's pecan pie (divine) and then showered off the day and put my clothes back on. It was six thirty. In a week, Daylight Savings would give me an hour of additional sunlight, but for tonight, I'd be working in the dark.

I clipped on Rocky's leash and took him out for a walk around the block. Porch lights, streetlights, and headlights illuminated the sidewalks enough to make the neighborhood feel safe. Rocky had been cooped up for most of the day, and a long walk filled with bushes to sniff and trees on which to pee was the least I could offer him.

The walk was uneventful. We returned to our block, but instead of going home, I went to my satellite office. Rocky trotted beside me, and when I unlocked the door, he led the way inside. He sniffed the boxes I'd left sitting in front of my desk and then went to his bed, a pink, donut-shaped pet cuddler. He curled up in the middle of the bed and promptly fell asleep.

I used a Swiss Army knife to open the packages and sort through the items. These were kitschy elements I'd ordered for use in the Mangieri ice cream parlor: long-handled spoons, aluminum cups for milkshakes, and vintage tulip glasses for sundaes. All items I'd purchased after taking the job. I cataloged each of them on my spreadsheet, logging in the amount spent and where they'd come from in the event they might have more to go with the finished product. But the more I looked at these accessories, the more I knew they were wrong.

When I designed a room, I started by asking the client to show me a favorite item in their existing décor. Often, it inspired my concept. But the Mangieris and I had bonded over the Orchid of Vincennes bathtub, and when I asked for an inspiration point, they said to go with my gut. I'd considered installing the fixtures from a now-defunct ice cream parlor which were era accurate simply by having been operated seventy years ago. That wasn't a design; it was fixture relocation.

In terms the bank would understand, the design didn't fit my brand.

My brain craved a break from thoughts of Olivia's murder, so I moved to my chair and grabbed a notebook. I jotted down words that reminded me of Paulie, Paolo, and their two children and then let my mind wander with ideas of an ice cream parlor like none I'd ever seen.

For starters, I'd scrap the idea of installing functional

soft-serve fixtures. Who wanted to deal with upkeep on vintage fixtures inside their house? I'd go with a cart. A gelato cart as a nod to Paolo's Italian heritage. I'd use my original concept of ice cream shades: cherry pink, pistachio, vanilla, and chocolate. For seating, I'd source out Nelson Coconut chairs. I'd recently acquired three from an estate sale buyout Effie had arranged, and I was certain I could turn up a fourth with minimal digging. The frames needed TLC, but a local powder coater could remedy that in an afternoon. Perhaps matte dark chocolate?

I grabbed a ring of SparkleLam™ samples from a new-ish company that replicated the look of glitter laminate countertops for the modern mid-century fan and flipped to the pink shades. I planned to install pink laminate counters flecked with silver and gold inclusions. For the floors, I would replace the wall-to-wall carpeting with a high-gloss checkerboard pattern. I'd obtained several boxes of stark white tile from a local contractor's yard sale and had attended a class at my favorite paint shop to learn how to paint and seal the tiles for high-traffic areas. If I could pull off a checkerboard pattern to match my color palette, the kids were almost guaranteed to love it, and I'd have a new skill to add to my ever-expanding repertoire of decorator tricks.

I filled two pages with notes about whimsical brass bowtie sconces—I vaguely remembered acquiring a set in a recent estate sale, but finding them amongst my inventory would require some digging—textured wall treatments to mimic coconut shavings, and glossy cherry-like bowls for the shelves, and then sketched it all out. I set my sketchpad down and sent an email to the Mangieris, thanking Paulie for his help at the commercial shoot and asking when the three of us could meet. I ended with a postscript hoping everything had worked out with Maggie and the mudballs. The thought of a little blond girl throwing mudballs at her schoolmates made me smile to myself. I sent the email and waited for a response.

SEVENTEEN

WHILE I WAITED, I GRABBED A SET OF COLORED MARKERS AND inked in the rendition. I had that familiar buzzing sensation inside my body, the feeling I got when I was so excited about an idea that I could hardly wait to start. I checked my email again, but still, there was no reply.

It had been a long day, starting at the pool, blurring into the furniture store set, then Nasty's visit, and finally working at my studio. I thought I'd dodged a bullet by not having to do the commercial live, but this was becoming the project that had no end! Now that I sat still, I felt the weariness that accompanies a marathon day. I swam regularly to clear my mind and manage the aches in my joints, but when I pushed myself like this, my previously injured knee responded with pain. It troubled me to think about the second day of filming. I needed to tell Virginia and Paulie about my limitations so they could help me when I needed a break. It would have to happen tomorrow, since I lacked Virginia's contact information and was still waiting for a response from Paulie.

I opened a separate internet browser and updated my spreadsheets with dates and locations of upcoming flea markets, but my attention span was starting to fade. I checked my email one last time and then closed everything out, woke Rocky, and headed home.

Ever since Tex and I started dating, first in private and then coming out to the world, we'd taken turns at each other's residences. His work as a police captain lent itself to odd hours and the occasional dangerous situation. Not long ago, I'd been at his place when someone broke in and stole a file, and the idea that it had taken place while we were enjoying a view of the stars from the rooftop deck had been unsettling for both of us. Thelma Johnson's house had become a safe space, but when he was in the thick of a case, his visits were short and usually with a purpose.

Tonight, it was just Rocky and me. I let us in and locked the doors behind us. The lingering scent of marinara permeated the air. My kitchen had seen more action in the past few days than it had in all the years I'd owned the house combined thanks to Tex's cooking. I was an adequate chef but found decorating to be a more fulfilling avenue for creativity and more often than not satisfied my food cravings with take-out from a local restaurant.

I rooted through various Tupperware in the refrigerator and found one with leftover rigatoni in red sauce. I doled a portion into a soup bowl, microwaved it, and sat down to eat. The savory flavor of the red sauce erased everything from my mind except for gratitude that Tex could make this. He'd been a bachelor for so long that he'd developed a unique set of survival skills including cooking, laundry, and wiring the lights in his living room onto a dimmer he controlled by remote. I tried not to think too much about the motivation behind that skill set.

I finished my pasta and cleaned up the kitchen. Tomorrow was trash day, and I'd missed the previous two weeks, so I couldn't let it go a third. I checked the bin under the sink and the second one in the pantry closet. Both were empty and lined with fresh bags. I turned out the outside light and pressed my face up against the window. Two large bins sat by the sidewalk, ready for pickup. I almost couldn't believe it. In addition to making a marvel of a dinner, Tex had taken out the trash. Was he going for boyfriend of the year?

Between the recap of the case and the Mangieris' ice cream parlor, I was alive with creativity and too keyed up to sleep. I decided to forego my morning swim so I could get an extra two hours in bed before I got to the set. I already knew it was a trade-off in terms of loosening up my body, but hadn't Virginia said something about hip rolls? I could enlist her to design a stretching routine to prep me for being on air. I switched off the lights, and Rocky joined me on the bed. I fell asleep before he settled into his spot.

Tortured dreams about dumpsters and ice cream stains filled my dreams. I woke with a start at four thirty-six. I was the opposite of relaxed. My heartbeat thumped in my chest and whooshed in my ears. All the details of my life were blurring together: decorating jobs, acting commercials, dumpster diving, and clues in the trash.

Clues in the trash.

I sat up straight. When the caterer threw her bags of trash into the bin, the bag had landed on top of a pile of rubbish and split open. I'd reached the cue card because it had landed on top of existing trash. But why was there a dumpster behind the abandoned factory? And why was it full? Arlene said she hadn't checked on the inventory in over a decade.

Surely Ling and Sue had looked in the receptacle when they secured the crime scene. Tex hadn't mentioned them finding anything, but he had recovered my fox-trimmed tweed jacket covered in motor oil from half a mile down the road along with the missing donuts.

I was now wide awake. I sat up and slipped my feet into pink leather Jacques Levine slippers. I took my robe off the back of my bedroom door and slipped it on then left Rocky snoring while I went downstairs.

It was pitch dark. In an hour, twilight would cast a glow to prep the city for daybreak, but right now, it looked like the dead of night. I was four hours away from my call time. Awake for now, but by the time the cameras rolled, I'd need a whole tube of concealer to hide the circles under my eyes.

I sat at the kitchen table and opened my laptop. This was the internet's job, to lull me into a mindless fog and distract me from my current worries. Perhaps solitaire would do the trick.

I played four games and then clicked over to email. There was a response from Paulie. I expected a reply regarding my design questions, but instead, I received an unanticipated message: *Madison—I have to cancel out of being your acting coach on the commercial. An existing client requires my help, and I must leave town unexpectedly.* He apologized for the late notice and said I'd be in good hands with Virginia.

Until now, I hadn't thought about Paulie's other clients and had assumed they were local professionals who found themselves in the unexpected position of being in front of the camera like me. But he'd aroused my curiosity, so I opened the internet and did a search for "Paulie Mangieri."

I got too many responses to sort through, so I added "acting coach" to my search and hit enter. The results narrowed down to a page that all said the same thing: *Local Acting Coach Gets Maximum Sentence for Car Theft.*

Paulie had spent time in jail? I dismissed any judgment. I'd once spent a night in jail, and I hoped anyone who dug up that tidbit would also find the details that explained why.

I scanned the article for Paulie's details. He'd stolen a white Mercedes SUV from the parking lot of a local entertainment venue. A club employee who was outside on a cigarette break notified the police, who were already there in droves. They caught up with Paulie less than a mile away. But for all the details about Paulie that I read in the story, the most interesting part was the very last line: *The stolen vehicle in question belonged to local performer Olivia Jean.*

EIGHTEEN

PAULIE WENT TO JAIL BECAUSE OF OLIVIA. PAULIE WENT TO jail because of Olivia. It was such an unbelievable connection that it played on repeat in my head. Paulie went to jail because of Olivia.

I read the rest of the article and then three more. Paulie had stolen an SUV from the parking lot outside Jumbos Exotic Dancers. Olivia was on a smoke break when she saw him break into the car and drive off. She went back inside and notified local police, who were already in the area. He was caught less than two miles from the club and held without bail.

There is no grand theft auto law in Texas. The laws that govern stealing a car, truck, or other motor vehicle fall under the state's other theft laws. The laws define penalty based on the value of the item stolen, not the category. That meant a sliding scale for the sentence.

A car valued under thirty thousand dollars would get a

state jail felony conviction. Over thirty thousand was a third-degree felony. Each sentence held a fine not to exceed ten thousand dollars, but the main difference was in jail time. A state jail felony meant up to two years in jail, but a third-degree felony was two to ten.

Paulie had been arrested for car theft twelve years ago. It didn't surprise me that the coveted car in question was an SUV; despite the flat terrain and mild winters, they were the car style of choice among Dallas residents. But a Mercedes cost more than a Ford, and that might have made a difference to Paulie's sentence. I read on and discovered the vehicle in question was valued at twenty-eight thousand. That meant Paulie's maximum sentence would have been capped at two years.

But the rest of the article proved me wrong. The car Paulie stolen had been recently customized with a three-thousand-dollar stereo that put the valuation at thirty-one thousand.

Paulie had been sentenced to ten years in prison.

I couldn't justify the man I knew with one who had served a ten-year prison sentence for stealing a vehicle. People change, but this felt like a radical shift. Ten years—that was longer than either of his children had been alive. Had he missed a part of their childhoods? Had this happened before he and Paolo met?

Did Paolo know?

I didn't ask my clients their ages. It seemed an unnecessary detail that was irrelevant to the job. But in trying to work out a timeline, I wished I had.

I grabbed a piece of paper and a pencil and did some

quick math. Paulie had said he spent the last fourteen years as an acting coach, and he said he and Jules went to the same University of Texas film program. But Jules was at least a decade younger than Paulie. A decade that, by my calculations, was unaccounted for.

I didn't have to think about what ten years in prison would do to a person. One night in jail had altered my perception. But why had Paulie stolen a car? What could have driven him to do such a thing?

I reread the email from Paulie. *I have to leave town unexpectedly.* The timing was all wrong. Last Friday, when he offered to help me, he'd said his schedule was wide open. Yesterday, after Olivia's murder, he'd been on set. On one hand, it felt safe. He hadn't joined the production until after the murder. He couldn't have been involved.

But on the other hand, there were too many things to connect him back to Olivia, things he hadn't told me. What if he'd followed her the morning of the murder? What if he snuck into the furniture store and stole my jacket—a possible disguise—while I introduced myself to Jules and then approached her in the parking lot out back, where they fought? What if he grabbed the nearest object—the coffee urn—to bludgeon her?

What if what if what if?

I had initially rejected Paulie's offer to help me, but he'd insisted. If he had an excuse to be at the store, volunteering to help me would explain his fingerprints if they turned up in the investigation. He would have discovered a room filled with potential suspects and could have written the new cue card himself to throw the case in a new direction.

Despite the saying that everything is bigger in Texas, in many ways, Dallas was a small town. It wasn't surprising to discover people who went to school together or who knew each other from intersecting employment gigs around town. Especially in my pocket of the city. It was the reason I accepted that Paulie and Jules knew each other from college. A person like me, who had moved to Texas in my forties, would always be an outsider. But for people who'd lived here their whole lives, the odds of running into an old friend were high.

Everybody has a past, I told myself. Everybody's done things they wish they hadn't. Everybody has a significant emotional event that colors their life from that point forward. Mine had been a breakup at the top of a ski slope, when someone I thought would be in my life forever told me he was married. I was light-years past that moment now, past hearing lies and learning the truth, but that moment stood as a detour sign in my life. It altered my course. That day, I skied away, hit a patch of ice, tore my ACL, and now lived with chronic knee pain. I uprooted my life from Pennsylvania to Texas. That moment made me aware of my limitations, but once I recovered and was mobile, it also made me value my independence. There was no way ten years in prison hadn't created a detour that altered the direction of Paulie's life too.

The bottom line: I had to talk to him. He was my client, my coach, and my friend. I replied to his reply: *Paulie, I know about your past. We need to talk.*

I received an automated out-of-office response.

GIVING the police a tip in an open investigation required them to follow up on it, which could cost them valuable time if the tip went nowhere. I didn't know what Paulie's past meant, but it wasn't my call. I sent Tex an email with four links and one line: *Is this anything?* And then I lay down on the sofa to rest my eyes for a moment.

I woke to the sound of the telephone. It took too long to orient myself to my living room, and by the time I answered, I knew I was late for the commercial shoot.

"Madison, this is Jules. Are you okay?"

"Jules," I repeated. My voice croaked out of me thanks to just having woken up. I cleared my throat and then added, "I'm on my way. I'll be on set as quickly as I can."

I arrived at Fraleigh Furniture forty minutes later. I'd forgotten to move the yellow dress from the icy water to the treatment phase of the stain, and when I'd checked it half an hour ago, the stain had set. Too late to do anything about it now, I wasted an extra ten minutes searching through my vast wardrobe of vintage dresses for a duplicate. It wasn't unusual for me to end up with more than one version of the same dress thanks to the popularity of Sears fashions from the sixties, but this time, I was out of luck. I turned up the same dress in white, green, blue, and pink. Even though I doubted Jules wanted to spend time and money color-correcting my wardrobe, I tossed the rest into my garment bag and left.

I burst into the store with Rocky by my feet. "I'm sorry I'm late," I said to Jules. She wore a version of yesterday's outfit: a baggy white T-shirt, torn jeans, black engineer boots. Her mirrored glasses were on top of her head, holding her disheveled hair away from her face.

She assessed me. "Aliyah is waiting for you," she said. "Go have her do your hair and makeup and change into the yellow dress from yesterday. I went through the footage, and what we got at the end of the day is usable. We can probably wrap early if we build on that."

"I left it at home," I said.

Jules didn't hide her irritation. She glanced down at Rocky, whose presence added to her annoyance. "You brought your dog?"

"I thought he'd add to the commercial. People love pets. He'll be cute. He'll make me seem more relatable."

"Can he act?"

I looked down at Rocky and then back at Jules. "He's a dog."

She shook her head. "We'll see how it goes."

There was no time to sleuth for the next two hours. Unlike yesterday, Aliyah was quiet while she got me camera-ready. The crew moved around, adjusting cables, lights, and furniture, talking among themselves but going silent when I was nearby. I tried to chat up one of the production assistants, who blatantly ignored me. If ever I needed a team of coaches, today would be the day, if only to make me feel less lonely.

As I buckled the self-belt on the blue dress, the door to the powder room opened, and Virginia came in. She had a cell phone up to her ear. She held her finger to her lips and then said, "I'm here with her now. Hold on." She handed me the phone.

"Hello?" I answered.

"I got your email." It was Tex. When he was on a case, he didn't waste time on hello. "Virginia said Paulie Mangieri didn't show today. Did you hear from him?"

"No," I said.

"If anybody asks, say you fired him. I sent Ling and Sue to his house this morning, but I want you to distance yourself from him."

"He's my client," I said. "I start demolition on his house next week."

"That job is on hold indefinitely. You hear me, Night?"

"Loud and clear, Captain."

NINETEEN

I HAD A HABIT OF USING TEX'S TITLE WHEN HE ANNOYED ME, and he usually annoyed me when we reached this state of police officer versus citizen. We reached this stage when his role as police officer *interfered* with my role as citizen, though he'd probably say the opposite. This time, the moment his title escaped my mouth, I recognized my error. Aside from Virginia, no one here knew the police were monitoring the commercial film shoot.

"I had to pull Clark from the set, but you've still got Virginia and Nasty. Do whatever they say, and keep your eyes open. I'm not ready to write off the crew as suspects just yet." He disconnected. I handed Virginia back her phone. She took it and remained in place, blocking me from getting to the door.

"We need to talk," she said. "Woman to woman."

Uh-oh.

"Sure," I said. "But is this the best time? I'm already late. Maybe we can chat after lunch?"

"Darlin, you have a problem," she continued as if I hadn't said a word. "The crew thinks you're a diva. I wasn't going to say anythin', but y'all took a long time in hair and makeup yesterday, didn't join them for lunch, and were unprepared on set, which cost them time. Now, you show up lookin' rougher than an alley cat. This was supposed to be a one-day job."

"Isn't that a good thing? The crew got a second day of work because of me."

"This isn't a high-paying gig. They're attached to this commercial and have to turn down other offers." She folded her arms in front of her. "And now today, you show up late. There's a lot of rumblin' out there, and in my experience, rumblin' leads to anger, and anger leads to hostility."

"I don't mean to be impolite, but is filming a commercial in a furniture store comparable to your experience?"

"You think I'm not acting when I get up on that stage?"

It felt like a rhetorical question, but internally, I knew she had a point.

Virginia's face softened. "Darlin', Tex asked me for a favor, and I'm here to deliver. He always looked out for us girls, and we feel like we owe him one. I may not look like a threat, but I'm a Texas girl, and I can open a can of whoop-ass better'n most. Right now, my job is to take care of you, and if you don't get your tush in gear, this whole operation is going to get shut down before it gets started. Know what I mean?"

"Sure," I said.

I didn't expect Virginia to actually act as my coach while she was here, but in terms of pep talks, hers was effective. I followed her out to the set. Jules was by herself behind the camera, while several other crew members clustered around Bruce a few feet away. The group around him was within her earshot, but she appeared to have tuned them out. If I weren't worried about her possible involvement in a recent homicide, I might have admired her ability to focus.

I crossed the room and went straight to Jules. "I'm here, and I'm ready. And I'm ready-ready. I know my lines, I know my marks, and I've got my secret weapon." I looked down at the floor, where Rocky sniffed her engineer boots. "I apologize for the delay this morning."

She glanced down at Rocky, and then her eyes rose and she took in my blue dress. Immediately, I recognized this as an opportunity. Instead of hiding what I'd done after yesterday's work, I used it to try to elicit a reaction.

"After we filmed yesterday, I helped the caterer take out the trash. I picked up a stain from the dumpster. I didn't treat it properly, and now that dress is out of commission. We're going to have to start from scratch."

Jules continued to stare at my dress to the point of discomfort.

I kept talking. "This is the same dress but in blue. The estate that I purchased it from—the original owner—had this dress in several colors. It fits well, and frankly, it's comfortable."

"Did you find anything?" she asked. It took me a few moments of silence to try to fit that question with what I'd been saying, long enough that she clarified. "In the dumpster. Did you find anything?"

I looked past Jules to the crew members who were hovering a few feet away. Most of them still watched Bruce, but Bruce watched me. I felt like I was in dangerous territory. If I gave away the clue of the cue card, I might tip someone off to my interest in the case, but if I lied, the caterer could just as easily spill the secret.

She continued. "Hudson told me how you drive around Dallas to find discarded treasures on trash day. It never occurred to me to go out back and see what someone might have thrown out. This place has been closed for business for decades, though, so I can't imagine there was anything out there...right?"

"Right," I said automatically. If Jules had been hinting around about the cue card, then she was cooler than a cucumber. "Right," I said again, this time with more conviction. "The only things I saw in the dumpster out back were from our shoot."

She nodded and then turned toward the crew. "Okay, people, we've got some time to make up today. Let's power through the morning and break for lunch at one." She scanned their faces and then looked at me. I smiled and got into position.

Jules peered through the camera while a PA moved around with a light gauge. When he stepped away, Jules looked up. "Do you want cue cards again today?" she asked.

"No. I rehearsed in the mirror last night, and I think I can get it."

There were snickers on set, but Jules didn't seem to

notice. "Okay. If you freeze up, I'll prompt you with a question. Just repeat the first part of the question back in your answer, and I'll cut my voice out in post."

I nodded. "Got it," I said.

"Great. Let's go, people!" she called out.

WE GOT through four full testimonials before we broke for lunch. Each time, Aliyah swept in to smooth my hair and touch up my lip gloss.

Nasty, dressed in a black suit and black stilettos, hovered in the background on her phone. Whenever someone approached her, she raised her hand and pointed to her earbuds. She was the most in-demand fake publicist Dallas had ever seen.

Virginia waited nearby, pointing to her smile when the cameras were rolling. She tried to get me to do hip swivels between the first and second takes, but I did a few pre-lap-swimming stretches instead. They sort of accomplished the same thing.

The distraction of the case seemed an effective way to keep me from worrying too much about my lines, and aside from one flub where I forgot the name of the police department, I did relatively well. Rocky joined me for the last one and stole the limelight. If Police Commissioner Fraleigh chose to air that version, I doubted any viewers would pay attention to my commentary.

Aside from commands of "Quiet on the set," "Roll sound," and "roll camera" or the ones uttered by the PA before clapping the slate, the only words I overheard for four hours were the ones I recited. After the second take on my fourth version, Jules broke for lunch. The male PA unlocked the store doors and let the caterers in. As various crew members made their way toward the front, Jules busied herself with the camera equipment. She seemed uninterested in mingling with the rest of the people there. Virginia handed me a robe to put on over my dress, and I told her to grab us lunch while I talked to Jules.

There was nothing about Jules that connected back to Olivia except for the fact that she was here the morning I found Olivia's body behind the store. But nothing else pointed to her as suspicious. I knew how the wrong-place-wrong-time crosshairs of a homicide investigation felt. It made her choice to distance herself from the others here make a little more sense.

I approached her. "Hi, Jules. Do you have a moment?" She kept her back to me and didn't turn my way. I was right behind her. "I wanted to talk to you about Paulie Mangieri." Still no response.

Jules was looking down at something in her hand, but her shoulder blocked my view of what it was. I couldn't have been closer to her without intimately invading her space, and it seemed clear she wanted nothing to do with me or my attempts at conversation. And the crew thought *I* was a diva!

"Jules," I said, this time with more force. I reached out and touched her shoulder, and she whirled toward me. Something small flew out of her hand and rolled behind a light-diffusing screen. She seemed alarmed but didn't retrieve the object in question.

"Madison," she said. "Did you need something?"

I glanced at the floor and pointed to where the thing she dropped had gone. "Was that important? Do you need to get it?"

"Trash," she said. She gave me a wry smile. "Don't tell the crew I littered."

Everything about her behavior felt suspicious. I'd been planning to ask her about Paulie, but a different question bubbled up to my lips. "Did you know Olivia?" I asked.

Jules's eyes widened. Her mirrored glasses were propped up, and this time, I saw surprise mingled with fear in her expression. She reached up to the top of her head, and I thought she was going to put the glasses on, but it appeared to be a nervous gesture to check that her glasses were where she'd left them.

"Yes," she said. "Why?"

I'd been hoping for more than one-word answers. "I was curious about her acting style and hoped you'd worked with her so you could give me pointers or something."

"I never worked with her. I met her under different circumstances."

"When?" I pressed.

Jules studied my face. Without the mask of her glasses, I could see her eyes scanning my features, focusing on my mouth over my eyes. It made her appear distant. She looked past me to the front of the store, where the crew and caterers had gone, and then slid her glasses down over her eyes. "It was a lifetime ago," she said. "It was a brief encounter, but not the type you forget." She pointed behind me. "You should get some lunch. We're going to have a busy afternoon, and I don't want you collapsing from hunger."

I nodded and started to walk away when she called out to me. "Madison, I forgot to tell you. Edward Fraleigh is coming to the set today. He was hoping to see a rough cut last night, but when I told him we were still shooting, he insisted on checking up on us."

TWENTY

THE SHIFT IN ENERGY THANKS TO THIS UNEXPECTED PIECE OF information was startling. Police Commissioner Fraleigh was coming to the set? Did Tex know? Without thinking, I glanced up toward the ceiling and scanned for Nasty's camera. If this was unplanned, then she'd get the message to him.

"That's great," I said, though, from the sound of my voice, I didn't sell my response as believable. "Are you going to get something to eat? Do you want me to bring you something?"

"No, thank you. I brought my own lunch."

I left Jules by the set and walked down the aisle of plastic-covered chairs toward the catering set-up. I'd been excited to go through the forgotten inventory, but already, it was fading into the background to a much bigger problem. About halfway to the catering setup, I turned around. Jules was on her hands and knees feeling around the floor for whatever it was she'd dropped.

Trash. Right.

I went to the powder room and dug out my phone. I didn't know where Tex was or who he was with, so the safer call was to the front desk of the police station.

"Lakewood Police Department," Imogene answered.

"Imogene, this is Madison."

"Hold, please," she said.

Immediately, I heard a perky, instrumental version of a song that took me several seconds to identify as Johnny Cash's "Folsom Prison Blues." Imogene had confided to me once that she replaced the police hold music with lullaby renditions of rock classics. I had to give her credit. In her way, she was making a change from the inside.

After several seconds, she returned. "Lakewood Police Department," she said again.

"Imogene! It's Madison."

"Hold, please." She clicked me over again. As impatient as I was, at least this time, I got to hear the rest of the song.

"Lakewood Police Department."

"Do not put me on hold," I commanded. I paused for a moment. When Imogene didn't say anything, I continued. "This is Madison. I have a message for Captain Allen."

"He's in a task force meeting. You want me to have him call you?"

"No. Just tell him Commissioner Fraleigh is coming to the commercial shoot today."

"I don't think so," Imogene said. "He was here at nine this morning, and he had his calls forwarded. The phones have been blowing up all day."

The door to the powder room opened, and Aliyah

entered. She glanced at me and then went into an empty stall. I left the powder room and hunkered down in the front corner of the store with my voice lowered. "Did you know Edward was going to be there today?"

"Hold, please." She clicked off but returned before I could place the next song. "Edward? Do you mean the police commissioner? Wow. I didn't realize you were on a first-name basis with him. Even Captain Allen uses his title. I think this commercial has gone to your head."

I turned toward the wall and cupped my hand around my phone. "I'm at the furniture store now, and it would be best if people didn't know I was in contact with the police department. Do you understand?"

"Oh!" she exclaimed. "Hold, please."

Johnny Cash returned, this time with "A Boy Named Sue." There was something about the Man in Black being replaced by a xylophone that made this conversation even more surreal.

Finally, Imogene returned. "Okay, I'm back. I forwarded the phones to the service and came out to my car so I can talk freely."

"I'm the one—never mind. Did your boss—you know who I mean, right?"

"Captain Allen?"

"Yes. Did he know Edward was going to meet with him today?"

"No. None of us knew. Ling and Sue had to give an update on the case. Sue wasn't happy. She said meetings like this cost them valuable time in the investigation."

Sue was right. Pulling the lead investigators out of the field this early was irresponsible.

Imogene continued. "I thought Captain Allen was going to take the meeting himself, but Commissioner Fraleigh insisted on having the two Sues there."

I didn't like it. Any of it. Why would he say he was coming to our film shoot? Or show up unexpectedly at the police station? If he wanted the case solved, why demand the investigators take a meeting instead of pounding the pavement and knocking on doors? It was like he wanted to interfere with the investigation instead of letting the police do their jobs.

Did Police Commissioner Fraleigh have a reason to keep Olivia's murder from being solved?

Paulie had left town unexpectedly, which brought his past connection to Olivia into the limelight. Now Edward Fraleigh was acting questionably. I needed two hands to keep track of the suspects on my fingers but none when it came to counting solid evidence.

Jules, Paulie, Aliyah, Billings, and now Fraleigh. Five people had either shown up unexpectedly or disappeared after Olivia's death. Aliyah had stood out as the most suspicious until I learned of Paulie's history with Olivia, but Commissioner Fraleigh's connection stood out too. He'd hired Olivia for this job, and this was his store. I'd never worked out why she was here the morning she died, but was there more to his wife's insistence that I take over the commercial spot than her love of my decorating style? Was there a dirty secret one of the Fraleighs wanted to keep from getting out?

"Do me a favor," I told Imogene. "Get a message to Captain Allen that I need to see him tonight. Tell him—tell him to meet me at the Rodeo Bar in the Adolphus Hotel. We should wrap here around five. I'm already in the area, so I'll probably get there first."

"I'll give him the message."

After disconnecting the call, I stood in my corner and watched the others.

Virginia mingled with the crew as if she'd known them for years. Jules sat by herself in a chair by the set. The caterers served food from the back of the table, and Rocky stretched his leash as far as he could to keep track of whether any of them dropped food.

Was there a killer here on set? Were those of us in the know foolish for showing up?

I scanned the room, looking for Aliyah. I hadn't seen her come out of the powder room yet, but it was likely that she left when I wasn't looking. I stood still so as not to draw attention to myself and tried to identify her in the room filled with people. She wasn't anywhere. I dropped my phone into the pocket of my dress and ducked back into the powder room.

I couldn't question Aliyah's motives for going into the powder room too closely; it *was* a powder room after all. I'd been in and out of it all day for reasons of my own. But Aliyah had that fingernail in her bag, and that made her suspicious.

The room was empty. I dragged my finger through the sink bowl. It was slick with water residue. There was a wad of brown paper towels in the trash, which would explain not having heard the hand dryer. I was too much of a lady—or at least too aware that I already had a bad reputation on set—to bang the stall doors open to check if they were vacant, but I bent down and looked for feet under each of them.

Aliyah must have left while I was on the phone. I stood in the center of the powder room with my back to the mirror. My garment bag still hung over the outside of the last stall, and Aliyah's black nylon gig bag sat on the floor in front of it.

My mind had turned toward other suspects, but I couldn't discount Aliyah based on that fingernail. If Nasty's hypothesis was true, the presence of the fingernail would indicate innocence. I had to see if it was still there.

I crept forward and picked up her bag. I propped it on the edge of the sink and held the sides wide open. In addition to a roll filled with makeup brushes and a transparent plastic bag of lipsticks, there were various styling wands and irons to both curl and straighten. I removed each item from the bag and set it on the windowsill, then pulled my phone out and used the flashlight just like yesterday. The fingernail was gone.

What did that tell me? Little more than that she'd cleaned out her bag. But if the fingernail had been a clue, it was no longer. Tossed in the garbage probably somewhere far away from Fraleigh Furniture and the site of Olivia's murder.

My phone rang from my pocket. I pulled it out and glanced at the screen. It was Nasty. I already knew what she was going to say, but I answered it anyway.

"Get out of the powder room," she said. "Now."

I should have listened. I should have accepted that sometimes, other people can see the bigger picture while we're too focused on individual pieces of the puzzle. Because while I lost valuable time preparing a retort, the door to the powder room opened, and Aliyah entered.

"Jules has me looking all over for you." She cut her eyes from me to her gig bag and then back to me. "What do you think you're doing?"

TWENTY-ONE

I DROPPED THE PHONE. ALIYAH STORMED TOWARD ME AND snatched her black bag from my hands. "You're going through my things?"

"I—I—" I couldn't think of a plausible excuse. Any answer that sprang to mind either incriminated me or her, and neither option seemed wise.

"Bruce was right about you," she said. She shook her head while rooting through her bag as if checking to see if I'd taken anything. "I thought you'd be good at this based on how your commercial turned out, but I guess you don't care about anybody but yourself."

I protested. "I'm as committed to this commercial shoot as I was my own."

"You show up late. Unprepared. You look like you were up all night. Why? You think those bags under your eyes are my problem, don't you?"

She kept ranting, and with each passing word, I felt less

and less confident about my role on the set. Nothing she said was wrong. I'd let my desire to help the police solve Olivia's murder get in the way of the one thing I should do while I was on set, which was film their testimonial. The reason I was here had nothing to do with my past success in solving murder cases; it was to help them with Tex's strategy of building bridges with the community. And I'd lost sight of that the moment I learned about their surveillance operation. I was ashamed of myself.

"Aliyah, I'm sorry. I know I look tired. I've been worried about us filming here. The police haven't arrested anyone for Olivia's murder, and we all just keep showing up and acting as if it never happened. I tried to sleep. I did. But I tossed and turned until close to five. I don't bounce back like I did when I was in my twenties. And now I heard the police commissioner is coming to the set to check on our progress, and I'm barely holding it together."

I couldn't help myself. As far as I knew, Jules hadn't told anyone else that Fraleigh was coming to the store, and according to Imogene, Jules's information wasn't correct. But just like telling Jules that I'd checked out the dumpster, I was pushing up against Aliyah to force a reaction. If she was hiding something, I wanted her to reveal it.

The makeup artist dropped her bag and leaned back against the door. "She wasn't supposed to be here," she said. "I took this job because they said she'd been replaced by you. After what happened at the airplane hangar, I never wanted to see Olivia Jean again."

I stepped forward. "Why?" I pressed. "A job is a job, right?

"You wouldn't understand."

The door behind her pushed in, and she jumped. The female PA stuck her head in. "We're ready to start filming." She pointed to my dress. "Jules said you had that dress in another color. Pick one and be on set in five minutes."

Aliyah followed the PA out. She turned back. "I'll touch you up on stage," she said and left me alone to change.

I picked the orange dress and was on my way to the back of the store within minutes.

Whether it was fear or guilt, my testimonials improved with each take. Rocky joined me from lunchtime on, and even Bruce seemed enamored of him. God bless the power of a Shih Tzu.

Like that morning, there was nothing to be overheard during the shoot. Everyone had one goal: get the commercial finished so we wouldn't have to come back for a third day. My goal was in opposition to theirs; the sooner we wrapped, the sooner the police lost access to the most likely band of suspects in Olivia's murder. No one had asked me to drag things out, but I was conflicted nonetheless.

At a quarter to four, Jules advised me to change once more. I took Rocky out front for a bathroom break and then went inside for one of my own, after which I traded the orange dress for the green one. I pulled my phone out of the pocket of the blue dress I'd started today in and checked for messages. Nasty's name was on the screen, and the counter was at five hours, thirty minutes, and counting. I raised the phone to my head. "Hello?"

"Hey," Nasty said. I was so startled to hear a voice that I

almost dropped the phone again. "When the makeup woman confronted you, you never hung up."

"You've been listening to silence for over three hours?" I asked.

"In the real world, people don't conduct business on a landline. You might want to invest in some earbuds and put your donut phone into storage."

"That's not the point. We've been filming for hours. Nobody even left to use the bathroom."

"Somebody did," she said, "But not like you think. While you were filming out front, someone went into the powder room, but they didn't use the facilities."

"How do you know that?"

"I heard them. Someone went into the bathroom and moved things around. I thought it was you. I expected to have this conversation an hour ago."

"What about your surveillance camera? Did you see someone come in here?"

"The cameras are set up by where you're filming."

"Can't you check that footage to see who wasn't on the set?"

"Not sure I'd know who was missing."

"I would," I said. "Let me review it."

"I'll email Tex the file after you leave for the day. Take it up with him."

She hung up. There were fourteen missed calls, which seemed an unusual number until I checked the first one and saw the name of my pool installer.

There was something distasteful about conducting business in a bathroom, so I went out front. I sat in a plastic-covered chair and listened to my messages, making note of each one. Jimmy reported in with an update: the fiberglass pool had been fitted into the excavated hole, and his team was plumbing and backfilling to make it stable. If all went as planned, he'd be done by the weekend.

This was the most exciting part of the project as far as I was concerned because while they fitted the skimmer box and installed the fittings, they would simultaneously fill the pool with water to provide equal pressure and stability. Until now, I'd had a hole in the ground. The pool wouldn't be finished until they reinforced the body and installed the deck, but after today, there was no going back.

Three of the missed calls were unknown numbers, and two were from Effie. The next eight were from Paolo Mangieri. I waffled between which call to return when one of the production assistants approached me. "Break's over. Jules wants you back on set."

"How much longer do you expect us to be?"

He shrugged. "Hard to say. We already got what we need, but Jules wants you to do a version in the green dress and another one in the pink, so it's up to you and how quickly you get through each take."

"What about Police Commissioner Fraleigh? Jules said he was coming, but I haven't seen him."

"His office called and said he was detained. They arranged for him to review the footage tonight." He checked his watch. "The sooner you nail this, the more time Jules has to cut something together for him to watch."

"Sure," I said. I put my phone and notebook back into my

bag and set them inside the powder room door. "Where will that screening be?"

He looked at me strangely. "Jules of Denial," he said. "Jules's production studio. Didn't you hear her announce it?"

"No," I said. "But I took my dog outside as soon as we finished with that last take."

He pulled out his phone and tapped quickly on the screen. I'd never get the hang of typing out messages with my thumbs, and every time I watched someone do it with extreme dexterity, I felt my age. "I just sent you directions."

"How did you get my phone number?"

He frowned at me. "We're on a job. I have everybody's phone number."

Like, duh.

I returned to the staging area and took my place. Jules called for last looks, which was when Aliyah stepped in, touched up my lip gloss, and smoothed my hair. There was no small talk or friendly encouragement.

The PA called out, "Quiet on the set!"

Jules said, "Roll sound. Roll camera. Speed."

The PA stood in front of me with the slate. Each time we did a take, he updated the information written on with a dry-erase marker: date, time, commercial title, and take. On a break, he'd explained that it was to organize various takes on a film shoot. Since we were recording different versions of me standing in one place, talking to the camera, he'd simplified and, after the date and time, wrote in the color of my dress.

"Green dress, take one." He clapped the slate shut.

Jules counted down, "Five, four, three," then she held up

her hand in a peace sign, and then just her index finger, and then she pointed at me.

"Hello, I'm Madison Night. I own a decorating business in the Lakewood/White Rock Lake area, but that's not why I'm with you tonight. I'd like to talk about our police department." Virginia stood behind Jules and pointed to her mouth. I responded with a smile. "I may not look it, but I've had plenty of opportunities to rely on the police department. You could say I'm their best customer."

I finished the thirty-second spot in twenty-seven seconds. We did another take with Rocky, and then I changed into the pink dress while the PA updated the slate. If all the involved parties were listening in, then they knew we were closing in on the final take of the job, and if they wanted me to stretch the job out for a third day, they were going to have to tell me soon. I almost regretted the quantum leap into competence I'd displayed today.

The final shoot was the best one yet. We finished at four thirty. I'd expected Jules to be the last one to leave, like a captain staying with the ship, but that wasn't how things worked in the world of film. She left first to review and edit what we'd recorded.

The staff, properly motivated with the end of a project, made short shrift of packing up the set. Even my suggestions that we leave things where they were "just in case" were met with bemused responses that all projected one word: Novice!

This was my last chance to observe the crew for suspicious behavior, and I wasted no time dawdling in the powder room. I held Rocky's leash tightly as people bustled around, unplugging cords, winding cables, packing up sandbags, stacking equipment on platforms with rollers, and moving it all out to a truck. They were a marvel of efficiency.

Even Virginia, who stood to my side, whistled under her breath. "When we do freelance jobs, it's a dancer and a portable boom box. Can you imagine the gigs we could book if we had a team like this to build and break down sets?" She grabbed my upper arm and leaned in. "I'm goin' to get Bruce's contact information." She scampered off toward the gaffer, fluffing her hair on the way.

After the crew packed up and the film equipment and the store had been returned to its original state, I led Rocky to collect my things. My garment bag and purse sat on the same plastic-covered chair I'd sat in earlier. I wasn't happy that my things had been moved out of the powder room. I unzipped my garment bag and peeked inside. The orange dress I'd worn two takes ago was missing. In my haste to change, I'd hung it haphazardly over a stall door, where it likely remained. Rocky, convinced we were on our way out the door, stretched his leash toward the exit and barked at the cars that pulled out of the lot.

"Not just yet, little guy," I said. I scooped him up and cradled him to my chest the same way Nasty had held her toddler, left my purse and garment bag in the chair, and entered the powder room, where Aliyah crouched on the floor, weeping into her hands.

TWENTY-TWO

By my count, we were the only two people left at the furniture store, though the PAs had to be around somewhere to lock the place up. I immediately set Rocky on the ground and looped his leash over the cold-water knob. I grabbed my orange dress from the stall door and spread it onto the floor like a picnic blanket, then lowered myself and sat next to Aliyah.

"What's wrong?" I asked.

"I'll never be free of her," she said. She inhaled in sharp gulps, each attempt to get air countered by sobs. Her long braids fell over her shoulder and bounced with each ragged breath.

"Who?"

"Olivia," she said. She bent down low and wrapped her arms around her head. Her back shook with erratic breathing, and her voice came out muffled. "I tried to get rid of her, but it didn't work."

"I don't know what she did to you, but Olivia can't hurt you anymore."

Aliyah raised her head. "But she can. She is." She wiped her eyes. "She's here. Right now." She looked up at the room. "Leave me alone! Let me be! Didn't you do enough already?"

What initially appeared to indicate an expedient confession devolved into behavior that made Aliyah appear unstable.

"Olivia is gone," I said. "We should be going too. I'll help you pack. The production assistants are waiting to lock up the store." I rubbed my hand on her back in a soothing manner.

"She said she'd ruin me, and she has. Ever since that stupid fight on set at the airplane hangar." Aliyah's sobbing subsided, but she was caught up in a narrative that only she knew, and I was getting a portion of the story. "I told her she couldn't have them. But then she complained about me to the director. I've never been unprofessional on a set, but it didn't matter. Denton fired me over—" She tried to take a breath, but it caught a few times and her body shook with each effort.

"What?" I prompted. "What did you and Olivia fight about?" My mind raced with guesses. A man? A job? A shade of lipstick?

"Fingernails," she said. Just saying the word sent her into a fresh wave of tears.

I suddenly felt cold. Did Aliyah know that I saw the broken fingernail in her bag? Or that I knew she disposed of it? Was this her admitting that she broke Olivia's fingernail in the struggle out back before she killed her? My heartbeat sped up, and I tensed.

Aliyah responded to my shift in energy. She dropped her hands and looked up at me. "You own a business. Do you know what it feels like when someone tries to steal what you built?"

We stared at each other. Fresh tears ran down Aliyah's dark cheeks. Her eyes were bloodshot, and her nose was puffy. Her glossy claret lip gloss had smeared around the edges of her lips. This was a woman who was trained in the art of cosmetic application, but right now, she was a mess.

The problem was it didn't seem like an act.

"I have some experience with stolen business ideas," I told her. My bad knee, bent too far for too long while I knelt next to Aliyah, couldn't take it anymore. I shifted my position and sat next to her on the tiled floor. "What happened between you and Olivia?"

Aliyah swiped away tears from her cheeks with the back of her hand. "I'm in the process of opening a nail art studio. I've been taking fewer film jobs, but Denton—the original director, you remember him?" I nodded. "We worked together on a job last year, and when he called me about these commercials, I said yes. He knew about my nail studio and said he'd direct a commercial for me as payment."

"Is that common?"

"No, but sometimes, when people are just starting out, favors are better than money. Denton's a successful commercial director. He knows what he's doing. I probably couldn't afford him otherwise."

I hadn't thought about Denton for days. When the

Fraleighs had the idea of me doing the commercial instead of Olivia, they'd replaced him with Jules. And after finding Olivia's body out back, everything had shifted toward the investigation. Denton hadn't been a part of this film shoot, so he hadn't even entered my band of suspects.

"Do you know why Denton was replaced when we moved the filming location to here?"

She sniffled. "He had another job already booked. The police offered him double pay to stay on, but he had to turn them down."

It took me a moment to realize when she mentioned the police, she was talking about them as a client and not referencing the undercover operation. I had to stay clear on the timeline because it was getting confusing.

Aliyah tipped her head toward the door. "Jules was a last-minute hire. Nobody here knows anything about her. I think this might be her first directing job."

The thought triggered me. From first meeting Jules at the furniture warehouse the day I'd found Olivia's body, I'd thought of her as Hudson's fiancé first, and the assistant director on the Pillow Stalking movie second. Despite her aloof attitude, I'd interacted with her differently because of those two facts. That wasn't to say that I thought she was above suspicion, but I'd bestowed upon her a level of competence she might not have.

All along, I'd acted as if she knew what she was doing, but if this were her first full directing job, she might not. And if someone knew that—if someone jeopardized this opportunity—she might not let it go.

I'd asked her about Olivia and she hadn't said they were

strangers. She'd said they'd met under different circumstances. How had I not heard the truth behind those words? Jules knew Olivia from something other than acting. What if Olivia showed up and threatened to ruin Jules' debut? Did Jules have it in her to fight for this opportunity, up to and including murder? And if that's who she was, did Hudson know?

I was brimming with questions, but none had to do with why Aliyah was crying inside the powder room. If I didn't take control of the conversation, I'd never remember it well enough to relay it to Tex.

"What happened with Olivia?" I asked gently.

"When I first got into hair and makeup, I worked part time at Jumbos. It gave me the chance to practice, and the dancers liked having someone to do their makeup each night. They paid me in cash, usually just tipped me out from what they made each night. Except for Olivia. She said the rest of them were foolish to pay me when I wasn't even licensed." Aliyah stared down at her hands and bit her lip. Crimson lipstick transferred onto her teeth, making her look like a recently sated vampire.

"At the airplane hangar, you told me she replaced you with her own hair and makeup team. That has to happen all the time, right?"

Aliyah looked up at me. "I lied. Olivia didn't have her own team. She told Denton she'd rather work with beauty school dropouts than with me and if he didn't fire me, she'd refuse to work and cost them money."

"I get why you wouldn't like Olivia, but why did she dislike you?"

"One night at Jumbos I—" she looked away and shook her head. "I can't say it."

"You have to say it," I countered. "Whatever it is, it's tearing you apart. What happened with Olivia at Jumbos?"

"It was my last night there. I landed a job at a small salon and the other dancers bought enough champagne to get me good and drunk in the dressing room. Toward the end of the night, I found myself alone with Olivia. She called me a loser with worthless qualifications and said the only way I'd succeed was if a director needed to fill a diversity quota on his team. Something in me snapped. I told her I would smooth out the back of her hair before her last set and I sprayed it with spray adhesive instead of hairspray."

"On purpose?"

Aliyah nodded. "It would have dissolved if she soaked her head in hot water, but instead of showering, she grabbed a brush and yanked it through—or tried to. The brush caught on the glue and ripped out a patch of her hair. I was so scared of what she'd do to me that I packed up my bag and left out the back door. I didn't think I'd ever see her again, but then there she was at the airplane hangar."

I didn't have to ask additional questions. From the first time I'd seen Olivia, I'd been struck by her gorgeous, glossy red hair. It made her look like a Vargas pin-up girl come to life.

"Did she say something?"

"She told me she'd get back at me. I had my nails done in my signature French manicure: pale pink with diamond shavings on the tips. It's the most expensive finish I offer. A lot of salons have a version with glitter polish, but I'm going for a top-end client. Nobody around here uses micro-shaved diamonds in their application."

I pictured Olivia lying in the parking lot. Her body was face down, and her arms were out on either side. Her left hand had long, pale, pink nails that sparkled under the sunlight. One nail had been missing, and I'd found that nail in Aliyah's bag. It had seemed so cut-and-dried, the clue that connected the makeup artist to the victim, but Nasty had been right. The presence of the nail didn't indicate guilt; the absence of the nail might.

I looked at Aliyah's fingers. Her nails were bare of polish and cut to the quick. A dull shine kept them looking healthy, but there was nothing about them that would make me think she was an expert manicurist.

She followed my gaze and balled her fingers up with each other in her lap. "I broke one," she said. "At the airplane hangar. Olivia complained about me to Denton. She said I was unprofessional and demanded he fire me. She didn't know about his and my arrangement, and he said he'd still do the commercial for me. I understood—she put him in a bad position, and he couldn't do his job if she wouldn't do hers." She shook her head at the memory. "I left the set that day. I was so angry at Olivia that I broke a nail getting into my car."

"Your nails weren't done when I was there," I said.

"This was the day before your commercial." She swiped at her eyes. "Good thing I saw it when it broke. Those nails cost a hundred dollars each. I threw it into my gig bag. When I got home, I took the rest of them off and put the set in my kit."

It sounded plausible enough, though I didn't think there was a way to check if her story was true. And I saw the fingernail in her bag yesterday, which was after she claimed she took it out. Something still didn't jive.

"You said Olivia tried to steal something from you," I prompted.

"She got my signature manicure from a competitor. She told them she got the idea from *D Magazine*, but she didn't. She got the idea from me. She stole it from me."

"Inspiration comes from a lot of places—"

"This wasn't inspiration. It was theft, plain and simple. She didn't just steal my idea; she stole my kit."

"Your makeup kit?"

"My manicure kit. I had it with me at the airplane hangar. I had an appointment that night and didn't want to risk not having time to get home to get my equipment. I had a fresh set of diamond-encrusted nails to use on a bride from a wealthy family, and when I got there, the kit was gone. I lost that job too. Two jobs in one day must be a record."

I knew the answer to my next question, but I asked it anyway. "Did Olivia know you found out what she did?"

"Yes," she said. "I was so mad. I had a friend call her and say the commercial had to be reshot and that we changed locations to here. I waited in the parking lot until she arrived, and I confronted her."

"What happened when she showed up?" I asked.

"We argued. Olivia waved her nails in my face. She said she was going to make sure everybody knew I was a fraud."

"Is that when you struck her with the coffee urn?"

"Is that how she died?" Aliyah asked. Her eyes widened. "Someone hit her with the coffee urn?"

I nodded. I didn't remember if that fact had been released to the public, but Jules, Bruce, and the two production assistants had all been on the set by the time the police arrived. Any one of them would have seen what I'd seen and would know what I knew. No one had advised me to keep it quiet, but Aliyah's response felt genuine.

Still, it wasn't a denial.

"You didn't hear about that on the news?"

"When I see her picture, I change the channel. I don't want to know anything about how she died. That morning, I said I hoped I never saw her again, and I stormed off. I circled the block twice and then went home. I wasn't even supposed to be here, so nobody noticed when I didn't show up."

"Aliyah, why did you say Olivia won't leave you alone?"

She looked me directly in the eyes. "You know how I told you I took off my fingernails and put the set in my kit at home?"

"Yes."

"Last night when I emptied my bag, there was another fingernail in there. An eleventh. I checked my set, and it wasn't one of mine. Don't you see? She's haunting me. Who else would do a thing like that?" Fresh tears filled her eyes. "She's making good on her promise to destroy me from beyond the grave."

TWENTY-THREE

BEFORE I COULD COUNTER ALIYAH'S ACCUSATION OF A GHOST, the door to the powder room swung open. The female PA jumped when she saw us. Rocky, who'd been quietly resting under the sink stood up and barked twice.

"We thought everybody was gone," she said. She seemed unmoved by Aliyah's tears or the fact that I was consoling her on the floor of the bathroom. "How much longer do you think you'll be?"

Aliyah pushed herself away from me and stood. She grabbed the handles of her gig bag and stood. "If Jules wants to reshoot anything, you'll need to find another makeup artist," she said. "I'm done." She left in a hurry and didn't say goodbye.

It took me longer to get up to a standing position than Aliyah thanks to my knee. When I was finally on my feet, I picked up my orange dress and dusted off the back of the pink one I wore. "I hope Aliyah was wrong about a reshoot. These dresses have a date with my washing machine."

"I'm fairly sure we got everything we need. We'll know tonight after Jules shows the rough cut to the client. You're all done in here, right? I need to lock the place up."

I unlooped Rocky's leash from the water faucet, and we went out front, where I collected my things. The production assistant locked the door to the store behind me.

"You got the directions, right?" she asked.

I reached into my pocket and checked my phone. There was a text message from the other PA, a missed call from Tex, and another missed call from Paolo. I looked back up and said, "Yes, it's right here. I'll see you tonight."

Rocky and I practically ran to the car.

Sticking around with Aliyah had kept me at the store for longer than I'd expected, but that conversation related to Olivia's murder and Tex's investigation.

On the bright side, if Tex were due at the rough cut screening with Police Commissioner Fraleigh and Jules, then I'd be able to get the men out to work on the pool installation without fear of being caught. What had started as a surprise had turned into one more ball to juggle, though for the first time since meeting Tex, I was thankful he had a murder investigation to keep him busy. I *did* feel guilt at that thought.

I checked my clock. It wasn't too late to return Paolo's call, but I wasn't sure what I'd say to him when I did. Three missed calls seemed excessive if he wanted to talk about the ice cream parlor. Chances were, Paolo knew where Paulie had gone and wanted to help cover his tracks.

The first call I made was to Tex.

"Where are you?" he said when I answered.

"I'm in the car. I just left the film shoot. You won't believe what just happened—"

"Are you close? I held a table for twenty-five minutes until the place filled up. They asked me to wait until my party arrived. Now the place is packed, and we'll never get a seat."

"A seat?" Oh, no! I'd forgotten all about my plans to meet Tex at the Rodeo Bar. "I'll be there in five minutes." I hung up.

It was the second time I was late today. I was less than two miles from the restaurant where Tex now waited for me, but it would take at least five minutes to navigate traffic, and I'd still have to find parking. I hoped the information I'd learned would make up for my tardiness.

I drove from the furniture store to downtown Dallas as quickly as possible and swung my car up to Valet. "I'm late meeting someone at the Rodeo Bar. Can you help me out?" I gave him my broadest Doris Day smile.

He admired my Alfa Romeo. "Sure, lady."

I grabbed both Rocky's leash and my garment bag and went into the hotel. They agreed to hold my belongings and watch Rocky while I dined. I regularly referred clients to the hotel when they needed a temporary place to stay during demolition and received benefits in the form of doggy daycare when I needed it.

The Walt Garrison Rodeo Bar had been a fixture in the downtown Dallas scene since 1981. It was the kind of place where people drank beer, ate burgers, and tossed peanut shells onto the floor. The restaurant had closed and rebranded as simply Rodeo Bar, and the patrons welcomed the reopening with the same gusto they'd reserved for the original. The décor was Early Americana with a heavy accent on Willie Nelson and whiskey.

The after-work crowd was now mixed with the early dinner crowd, and that left a packed restaurant and an annoyed Tex staring out the window by the street-side entrance. I still wore the now-filthy pink dress from the photo shoot and far more makeup than usual. The crowd parted to let me through, and I reached Tex before he saw me coming.

I put my hand on his shoulder. "I'm here," I said.

He turned around and surveyed me from head to toe. His angry expression softened, and I considered leaning in for a kiss. Someone bumped me from behind and knocked me into Tex, who made no effort to push me away. I looked up at him and apologized.

"I know you don't like that I'm late, but you're going to love when you hear what kept me there."

He raised his eyebrows. "This better be good, Night. I'm starved, and there's a forty-five-minute wait."

I turned around and looked at the hostess. She was a thirty-something woman with hair so blond it was almost white. She tapped the screen in front of her and cued up a display of tables.

"Excuse me," I said, leaning closer to her to be heard over the din. "My party was seated but gave up his table when he found out I was detained." The woman stared at me. "Can you tell me how long the wait is for a table for two?" I added. I smiled and leaned to the side so she could see Tex too.

"You're that woman from the commercial," she said, "the decorator who repurposes stuff from the trash."

"Yes, I am," I said.

"You wear the best clothes," she said. She stepped back and studied my dress. "Gorge." Her eyes traveled down past the hem to my green Keds, and her eyebrows drew together.

I leaned close and said under my breath, "They make it easier to dumpster dive for treasures." I leaned back and smiled again.

Her expression changed from consternation to understanding, like we were co-conspirators. "I keep a table for celebrities. Come with me."

I turned toward Tex to see if he'd overheard. He rolled his eyes.

The waiter stopped by with a basket of shelled peanuts and a pair of menus. Tex ordered a beer, and I ordered a club soda. The waiter promised to return shortly and disappeared into the crowd.

Tex's hands were on the table. I put my hand on top of his. The circles under his eyes were as pronounced as they'd been the last time I saw him. "Did you sleep at all last night?"

"Wojo got into the pantry and knocked over a bag of semisweet chocolates."

"Is he okay?"

"He'll survive. I heard the crash and got to him before he tore the bag open."

I pressed my lips together to stifle a smile but was only

marginally successful. Rocky hadn't sniffed out chocolate when he was a pup, but he'd had a habit of knocking over lamps. "How's he today?"

"Contrite. And empty. I didn't know a dog his size could produce that much of a mess."

"You could have called me. Rocky was no angel when he was a puppy. I've been through it all."

"Night, you're my girlfriend, not my maid. I don't need you to handle my dog's bowels."

"Is there something you do need me for?" I asked playfully.

"Yes." He flipped his hand over and cradled mine in his. His palm was soft and warm, and his fingers were callused in places from firing a gun. I felt safe with Tex in a different way than I'd felt with other men in the past. He treated me as an intellectual equal and knew I could take care of myself—most of the time. And while I knew Tex was responsible for the protection and safety of an entire community of people, I knew when I needed him, he'd be there for me.

"What?" I asked. My voice was low, inviting a response that erased the image of Wojo's digestive tract from my imagination. I'd found the most intimate conversations with Tex often took place in public. It was an after-effect of keeping our relationship secret for so long. Clandestine touches and whispered flirtations had been the foundation of our early attempt at dating, and it had been exciting. Neither one of us had expected our work lives to cross over like they were now thanks to the commercial, but it had been easy to slip back into old habits of professional appearances. "What do you need from me?"

"Your willful acceptance of my past," he said. He raised my hand to his lips and kissed my fingers. "And your storm cellar."

Between placing our order and eating our burgers (there was no point ordering any of the other options on the menu), I filled Tex in on my conversation with Aliyah. At times like this, I could count on him listening and interrupting to ask pertinent questions, making expedient the process of relaying information.

"Do you think she was acting?" he asked. "The whole woo-woo, Olivia's-haunting-me thing?"

"No," I said honestly. "I thought about her the whole way here. She and Olivia have a past and it's not pretty. If Olivia was the type to hold a grudge, which she seems like she was, then Aliyah was right to worry. Aliyah was freaked out by the fingernail she found in her bag last night."

"The timeline is that she did her nails, then Olivia saw them and wanted a set. Aliyah refused, and Olivia got her fired. Aliyah then arranged to meet Olivia on the new set to have it out, and Olivia showed up with a full set of Aliyah's signature nails done by someone else and threatened to tell the world Aliyah is a fraud."

"According to Aliyah, she broke a nail after Olivia got her fired and removed the full set. She said they cost a hundred dollars each. She put the broken one in her bag and removed the set when she got home that night."

"Which means—what?"

"She thinks it means Olivia's ghost planted a fingernail in her bag."

"What do you think?" Tex asked.

"Aliyah admitted to being at the set the morning Olivia died. She admitted to being the reason Olivia was there, and she admitted to having a motive." I stopped to take a sip of water. "But I don't think she did it. When I asked her when she hit Olivia with the coffee urn, she denied it."

Tex had raised his beer to his lips, but he stopped with the glass midway. He put the glass back onto the table. "You asked a person of interest if she committed murder?"

"We were two women talking in the powder room. Aliyah was upset, and I consoled her. That fingernail has been bothering me since I first saw it."

"Nasty said *she* found the fingernail."

I knew conspiring with Nasty was going to come back to bite me!

"She told me to let her take credit."

"Nasty is on the payroll. She's an independent contractor hired by the police force to aid in an ongoing homicide investigation. She's required by the terms of her contract to report to the department. You, on the other hand, have no legal or contractual connection to this investigation."

"Your boss's wife asked me to do this. I accepted an envelope of cash as payment. Surely there's some sort of case to be made that I'm on the payroll too."

Tex raised his glass to his lips and finished the contents. After he swallowed, he set the empty on the table and stared straight at me. "How long until this commercial is wrapped?"

"Hopefully, we're done. Are you going to the rough-cut viewing tonight?" I asked. Tex stared at me with a blank expression on his face, so I continued. "Commissioner Fraleigh wants to see the commercial. Jules was the first person to leave the set so she could put something together to show him. One of the PAs texted me details. You weren't told?" He shook his head. "You should be there. Come as my date."

"No," he said.

"This is no time to stir up your alpha-male tendencies. I'm simply suggesting a convenient excuse to get you to a site that may help with your investigation."

"Oh, I'll be there, but you won't. If there's something going on, I want you as far away from it as possible."

Before I had a chance to protest, declare my independence, or refer to him as my least favorite relic of the mid-century era, he reached across the table and took my hand.

"You're on that site as a favor to me. We agreed that if things got too dangerous, I was going to pull you out. I appreciate the risk you took, but I don't like the fact that nobody told me about this screening."

I relaxed my hand into Tex's. Everything he said was true, right, and accurate, and this wasn't like the past.

"Don't you think it'll seem odd if I don't show?" I asked.

"You've been neglecting your business," he offered. "I'll offer your apologies and tell them you had a late-night meeting with a client."

It was a promising idea, and technically, it wasn't a lie. Because with my newly freed evening, I intended to pay a visit to Paolo Mangieri.

TWENTY-FOUR

THERE SEEMED NO POINT IN ASKING TEX TO FORWARD ME THE surveillance footage Nasty sent him. His response to issues of this nature was remarkably consistent. I forwarded the details about the rough-cut viewing to Tex and then we finished our burgers with non–homicide-related conversation and paid the bill. On our exit from the restaurant, I handed out four business cards to strangers who inquired about Mad for Mod. Overall, it was a productive respite to a week of drama.

It was late enough that traffic had subsided. The temperature had dropped, and there was moisture in the air. The news had called for rain, and it felt like a storm was due any minute.

I checked in with Effie from the drive. I trusted her with Mad for Mod, but I liked daily updates.

"Hey, Boss," she answered. "How's the acting gig?"

"Fine," I said. "I think we might have wrapped today."

"Listen to you with the lingo. Next thing you know, you'll have a star on the Hollywood Walk of Fame."

"If they recognized decorators, I might lobby for one." I shared a laugh with her and then inquired about the business.

"Everything's fine," she said. "I paid the invoices that came due and hid the file on your pool in case Captain Allen comes here unexpectedly. There's a pair of damaged Poul Jensen Z chairs on 1stDibs. They want a thousand for the set. You want me to contact them?"

"How damaged is damaged?"

"They're missing their cushions, and one of them has a broken leg."

"I acquired three in similar condition in an estate-sale buyout that you have yet to catalog into inventory. Let someone else have them as a weekend project."

"You got it."

We finished with a few extraneous business details. "I'm not sure if I'll be in the office tomorrow," I said. "Captain Allen will be busy with work tonight, so I'm going to see if I can get work done on the pool."

"What about the ice cream parlor?" Effie asked. "The way Paolo's been burning up the phone here, I figured you'd be there as soon as you could."

"I'm headed there now."

"Then I'll let you go. See you tomorrow, Boss!"

Effie didn't realize it, but she'd taken my anxiety over returning Paolo's call and converted it to extreme curiosity. It made sense that he might blow up my cell phone, but to try to reach me at the office too? That didn't fit. Not if this was about covering Paulie's tracks.

I took an exit, drove toward the Hillridge neighborhood, and parked out front of the Mangieri residence about ten minutes later. Paolo's bakery truck was in the driveway. Was this a bad idea? I didn't want to think that it was. Before Olivia's murder, I'd considered the Mangieris not clients but friends. I wasn't willing to believe I'd been that wrong about my assessment.

I clipped on Rocky's leash and led him to the entrance. As if further evidence that the Mangieris and I were cut from the same cloth, they'd spent their weekends digging through salvage yards until landing on the perfect front door. A thorough sanding and a coat of cherry-red paint freshened it up. The doorbell was nested into a chrome starburst escutcheon. I pressed the button and heard chimes inside. Moments later, the door opened, and Paolo greeted me. He held Maggie with one arm. His black hair stood on end, and his five o'clock shadow had turned to scruff. A smudge of flour was on his cheek.

"Madison." He tapped Maggie on the back and kissed her cheek and then set her down and told her to go play with her brother. She ran off into the living room, and he invited me inside. "Have you heard from Paulie?" Paolo said something in Italian that reinforced his already agitated state. "He didn't pick up the kids from school today, and he hasn't returned any of my calls. Do you know where he is? I am so worried. This is not like him to just disappear."

"Paolo, calm down. I'm sure Paulie is fine," I said, sure of nothing.

"He is gone. Into thin air. I don't know what to tell the children. I don't know what to do!"

Paolo's concern was palpable. I followed him through the area that was to become the ice cream parlor into the kitchen. A mess of baking equipment covered the counters, along with industrial-sized canisters of flour, sugar, baking soda, and something green. A bottle of vanilla extract so big it looked like a funhouse prop was on the island next to hinge-top glass canisters of colored sugar. Willy Wonka had nothing on Paolo Mangieri.

"It's going to be okay," I said automatically, though a tiny part of me had seen enough by now to know that maybe it would not.

"He left us," Paolo said. "We got into an argument on Monday night after we put the children to bed. He stormed out and hasn't returned. I've called him a hundred times, and it always goes to voice mail." He was visibly upset.

A bell went off, and he turned his back on me and opened the door to the oven. A sweet cloud of sugar and vanilla wafted toward me. Paolo slipped on an oven mitt and pulled out two trays of cookies sprinkled with colorful sugar granules and set them on cooling trays. He closed that oven and opened the one next to it and pulled out two more trays. Paolo's kitchen was bigger than my bedroom, and now I could see why.

He left the kitchen and returned with two trays of unbaked cookies that he slid into the ovens. I waited while he closed the door and set the timer.

"This must be a trying time to have a catering job," I said.

"There's no job. When I get upset, I bake." He picked up

a sifter and poured some flour into it and then stopped. And stared into the bowl. And then picked up the bowl and tossed it against the wall.

Dusty white flour particles filled the air and coated the countertops. I stood close enough that a layer of flour clung to my blue dress as well. Paolo bent down and put his face in his hands and remained there for a few seconds before standing up.

"I took a leave from the bakery so I can take care of the kids," he said. "I think he has left us for good."

"Paolo, let's go sit down." I led the pastry chef into his living room. We sat on a fluffy pink sofa that had nothing mid-century modern about it but was durable and stain-resistant, two necessary qualities for parents of rambunctious children. "The last time I saw Paulie was at the commercial shoot. He had to leave early. He said the school called about Maggie throwing mudballs at another student, and you couldn't get away. That was yesterday."

"That is all true. He came home from your commercial in a bad mood. I asked what happened, and he said he couldn't talk about it. I said he could tell me anything, we were life partners, but he said not this. It was his past, and he said I wouldn't understand. Do you know what happened?"

"I told you what I know. He was there, and then he had to leave suddenly. I didn't think anything of it at the time."

Since then, I'd learned about Paulie's background, but judging from what he'd told—or rather, hadn't told—Paolo, the information I'd discovered wasn't common knowledge within the walls of the Mangieri house.

"I should have given him his space, but I could not. I am

embarrassed by my behavior. I hate that I am such a jealous man." He rested his elbows on his knees and put his head in his hands. He shook his head and then, in a voice that was difficult to hear, said, "I accused him of having an affair with the director."

"With Jules?" I asked. Paolo nodded. "But Jules is a woman," I said.

Paolo sat up and looked at me. "He said it was something from his past. Something I wouldn't understand."

It was clear to me that whatever was going on with Paulie, Paolo didn't know. Here was a distraught husband overcome by guilt over saying the wrong thing in the heat of an argument. "I was on the set the entire day that Paulie was there, and I can tell you there's nothing between him and Jules. They acted like two people who knew each other and worked together. Paulie loves you. He loves your family. He will come back."

Paolo leaned forward and grabbed both of my hands. "I want you to continue your work on the ice cream parlor," he said earnestly. "I trust you completely. I want him to have whatever he wants."

I made him promise to call me when Paulie came home. Paolo agreed, and we said goodbye. I conveyed confidence that Paulie would return, but inside, niggling doubts ate at me. I didn't know the full extent of Paulie's troubles, but abandoning his family was a clear indication of guilt.

TWENTY-FIVE

IT WAS A HOP, SKIP, AND A JUMP FROM THE MANGIERI residence to Thelma Johnson's house, and my thoughts were so crowded I arrived at the house without remembering the drive. I'd been going-going-going since this morning. I'd barely stopped for a breath. If not for my burger with Tex at the Rodeo Bar, I might not have remembered to eat.

Rocky followed me to the garage while I checked on the state of the pool installation. I was impressed by how the contractors had been able to work within the confines of the garage walls. They'd driven the Bobcat through the garage door to dig the hole, temporarily relocated the roof to the back of a flatbed truck while they lowered the fiberglass pool body into the ground, and then set replaced the roof to keep their progress hidden.

I unlocked the side door to the garage and switched on the temporary lighting that had been rigged overhead. The progress was astounding. What had once been a two-car garage with a workbench, pegboard, and a slew of old tools left behind by Thelma Johnson's husband had been replaced by an eleven-by-twenty-five-foot rectangular in-ground pool. Not only was the pool filled with water, but Travertine pavers had been installed around the perimeter, a step I'd been told was both functional and flattering. The paver coping covered the rebar and was reinforced with concrete. The rest of the ground was covered in loose gravel.

I fed Rocky and called Jimmy.

"Hey, Madison. I've been hoping to hear back from you today. We finished installing the rebar and the pavers. The only thing left is to install the deck. Once we finish that, it's all yours."

"How long will that take?"

"I've got the concrete blocks at my store. It won't take more than a couple of hours to install them, but when is the problem. My daughter's dance recital is tomorrow night, and my son's football game is the day after. We're looking at three days out at the minimum."

I left the garage and walked toward the house. I was in the middle of projects with no completion dates, and the lack of forward progress was weighing me down.

"What about tonight?" I asked. I remembered the envelopes of cash Drew Billings had given me to film the police commercial—money that didn't feel like it belonged to me despite having been told to keep it. "There's a five-thousand-dollar cash bonus in it if you can make that happen."

"Hold on." I heard a muffled sound on the other end of the phone, and then Jimmy returned. "Assuming Mother

Nature doesn't open the skies on us, you got yourself a deal. I'll rally up a crew, and we'll be there within the hour."

I thanked Jimmy and went back into the house. Rocky was in the living room, nuzzling a furry ball with his nose. I turned on the TV and clicked to the local news channel to check the weather. The rain wasn't expected to start until somewhere around midnight. I hoped this was one of the rare nights when the meteorologists were right.

I went into the kitchen and pulled three twelve-cup electric coffee pots out from the cabinet under the sink, measured out coffee, and filled them with water. In the background, the local reporter said there were no updates in the murder of Olivia Jean. The man's voice continued with a summary of what the police—and the public—knew by now: the victim, a performer who worked at Jumbos Exotic Dancers in the Casa Linda Plaza, had been found dead outside an abandoned furniture store in the design district.

"Sources at the site informed us that Ms. Jean had recently been replaced on a commercial shoot for the police department. Police are investigating several leads and hope to have someone in custody shortly."

I left the kitchen and went to the living room to turn off the TV, but the image of Tex stopped me. He was at a podium. The two lead officers on the case, Ling and Sue, stood to the left of him. Tex had on a suit and tie, and his hair was combed back away from his face. He looked tired.

"Ms. Jean was not working for the police when she was murdered," he said.

A voice called out a question from the audience of the press conference. "Was she fired?"

"After a test screening of her commercial, the department decided to go a different direction."

"Wasn't Olivia Jean a dancer at a cop hangout?" another voice called out. "Did you have a personal relationship with the victim?"

Tex looked uncomfortable. "Ms. Jean has worked a number of jobs in the Dallas area. She was a resident of this town, just like you."

"Is it true someone stole a box of donuts from the crime scene?" the reporter persisted. "Do you think that was a jab at the police?"

Next to Tex, Ling and Sue looked at each other. Those donuts had been missing and found within hours of the murder. Who leaked that information to the press, and why was it coming out now?

Tex put his hands on the sides of the lectern and gripped hard. I knew his body language, and I knew the question left him angry. The whole point of the commercial was to color the police in a positive and helpful light, not a punchline.

"Thank you. This press conference is over." He pushed away from the lectern and walked away. Ling and Sue followed.

Tex had spent the past year recruiting to fill his open officer positions and had changed the face of the department. Ling and Sue had been part of that recruitment effort, and their success rate on confessions had given the Lakewood PD national recognition. Their meme: YOU'VE BEEN SUED! written over a stock image of a man in handcuffs was the most-liked post from the department's social media feeds.

Ever since taking over as captain, Tex had struggled with the perception of the department as an authoritarian rule. He'd sent his officers out into communities to get to know the residents when there was no trouble so those residents would feel more comfortable calling when there was. He wanted people to know the police were there for them, but this reporter was going out of his way to make it sound like Olivia's involvement with the police was what had gotten her killed.

I spent a few minutes playing with Rocky while my mind buzzed. The scent of freshly brewed coffee ballooned through the house, and when Rocky tired of our game, I went into the kitchen to prepare a tray to take outside. Within half an hour, a truck pulled up outside.

I left the coffee in the kitchen and went to the garage with Rocky by my ankles. He ran to the edge of the water and sniffed. Jimmy climbed out of the truck with a man who was a younger, puffier version of him. They both wore baseball hats, oversized hoodies, and jeans. Jimmy's hat was green, and the younger man's was blue.

"Hey, Madison. This is my son, JJ. I'm training him to come work for me when he turns sixteen. He's been helping with your installation." The two of them joined me outside the garage. "What do you think?"

"It looks fantastic. When this job is over, you have to give me a stack of business cards to hand out to my clients."

Two additional trucks showed up, and several muscular men got out. A flatbed loaded with rectangles of concrete pulled up behind the last of the trucks and parked.

"So, how long we got tonight?" Jimmy asked.

"How long do you need?"

Jimmy put his hand on the bill of his baseball hat and held it in place while he looked up at the sky. "The job'll take two hours. Let's hope the rain holds off that long."

"Done. I'll set up a coffee station."

I called Rocky back to me, and we went inside while the men got to work. The beauty of installing a pool inside a two-car garage was that the garage doors served as an easy entrance. I leaned on the windowsill inside my kitchen and watched the construction crew carry the concrete into the garage in shifts. By the time the coffee was ready, the bed of the truck was empty.

While Jimmy's team worked on installing the concrete deck, I set up a card table outside the garage, covered it in a vinyl-laminate tablecloth printed with colorful graphics by Vera, and brought out coffee, sugar, creamer, and mugs. I didn't particularly want to encourage the guys to dawdle, but they were working beyond the call of a regular workday, and a little generosity seemed in order. I added a box of Entenmann's hot cross buns to the table next to a stack of mismatched melamine dishes I'd acquired over the years, took a bun for myself, and went back inside.

The construction crew had set up bright lights around the garage doors to help illuminate their job site. Another truck arrived. I had no idea how many men it took to install a pool!

The new arrival got out of his truck and strode toward the house. He was backlit by the lights from the garage, though I could tell by his build that he was leaner than either Jimmy or his son. As it became clear that the man was coming my way, I stepped away from the windows but kept an eye on him. I shouldn't have felt nervous. There was enough muscle a hundred yards away from me to install a pool in under a week. But the closer the man got, the stronger my sense of recognition became.

And by the time he pounded on my front door, I knew.

It was Paulie Mangieri.

TWENTY-SIX

THERE WAS NO POINT HIDING BUT ALSO NO POINT TAKING unnecessary risks. I grabbed a carton of Cinnamon Toast Crunch–flavored nondairy creamer from the fridge, an accidental purchase that had remained both unopened and refrigerated in case of creamer emergencies, and went to the door.

"Paulie, this is a surprise." I stood in his way, blocking the entrance to my house.

"I need to talk to you," he said. He glanced behind me as if checking to see if I were alone. "Can we go inside?"

"I was just on my way to take this to the workers." I held up the creamer. "Walk with me?"

He looked over his shoulder toward my garage and seemed unhappy with my suggestion, but, barring any alternatives, stepped backward and then down my steps. I pulled the front door closed behind me so Rocky wouldn't get out, and I joined him on the sidewalk.

"Your husband is upset," I said. I squeezed the nondairy creamer as if it were my lone method for protection. The only thing I knew about Paulie, aside from what he'd filled out on his client profile, was what I'd read online. I wanted to trust him, and I'd give him the benefit of the doubt—for now. "You need to tell him you're okay."

"I can't," Paulie said. "He'll want to know where I went, and I'll have to tell him everything. I'll have to tell him about what I did, and he'll see me differently. We might lose the children. I ruined my own life, but I can't bear to ruin his and theirs too."

We reached the table with the coffee pots, and it occurred to me that if Paulie had indeed bashed in Olivia's head with a coffee urn, he might react to seeing three set up here. I glanced past him and caught JJ watching me. I forced a smile that did more to project my fear than my confidence. His dad called to him, and he looked conflicted. But Dad took precedence over me, and JJ walked away.

I set the creamer on the table. "Would you like a cup of coffee?" I asked Paulie. "I brewed it for the construction crew, but there's plenty."

"I'd love one." Paulie reached across me for a cup and poured hot coffee into it. Steam rose from the top, and a strong, bitter aroma blossomed in the night air. Paulie looked at the Cinnamon Toast Crunch nondairy creamer and then set the coffee cup down and started to cry.

I'd had an emotional response the day I realized I bought the wrong creamer too, but it hadn't been tears.

"Paulie, what's wrong?" I asked.

"That's Maggie's favorite," he said. His face was slick

from crying, but I could tell he was working to keep his emotions in check. "What have I done?"

"Follow me."

I led Paulie to a vintage metal outdoor swing toward the back corner of my house. The seat was covered in plastic-coated vinyl, which made it impervious to weather. Last year, a friend had helped me sand off the rust and repaint it. It was right around the time I'd been enrolled in business school and had gotten the idea to expand Mad for Mod. When another friend who'd recently purchased a flower shop returned from a landscaping show brimming with ideas, I offered up my backyard as her canvas. The resulting scene represented both of our businesses, so we split the cost of a professional photographer and shared the images in our respective portfolios.

I sat on the swing and gestured for Paulie to join me. He sat down, and the metal chains that suspended the swinging seat creaked with our weight. He put his hand on the support bar and ran his open palm up and then down as if it were covered in velvet and not coated in dirt.

"Paulie, I know about the car theft," I said. "I know you spent time in prison."

"How did you find out?"

"I looked you up online." I waited for him to deny it or make up an excuse, but when the silence stretched out between us, I continued. "I'm not in the habit of doing background checks on my clients, but I had no idea you were an acting coach. After you said you couldn't make it for the second day of the commercial shoot, I thought it was because you already had a more important client. I looked up 'Paulie Mangieri acting coach,' and the articles came up."

"When I volunteered to help you, I had no idea you were hired to replace Olivia Jean on the set. I honestly thought working with you would be fun. But that first morning, I heard the crew talking. I asked around, and when I heard her name, it all came back to me. I had to get out of there before someone put us together and thought I was involved."

"That's why you left to pick Maggie up from school but never arrived."

He sat against the back of the swing with his neck bent forward. His hands were now folded in his lap, and he ran his thumbs in circles around each other.

"Paolo doesn't know, does he?"

Paulie shook his head.

"How is that possible?" I asked. "You two are inseparable. Andy is almost six, and you adopted him when he was a baby. I don't know what happened to make you leave, but whatever it is, you have a family that will stand by you."

"This has nothing to do with them."

I turned to face him. "You have to tell him. You have to trust that he loves you, the you that he's known all along, and that he'll accept whatever happened to you in your past. He cares about you. He's worried sick."

Paulie snapped his head up and looked at me. "You talked to him?"

"He thinks you abandoned him. And the children. He said you had a fight and you walked out and that he wasn't worried until the school called and told him to pick up Maggie and Andy."

Paulie stared at me. His lips were pressed together in a tight line. "Did I ever tell you how I met Paolo?"

"No," I said.

"It was in Italy. After...after." He lapsed into silence and stared at his hands then balled them into fists and pushed them into the pockets of his windbreaker. "I went by myself. I needed a fresh start, and I didn't know where it was going to come from. Turns out it came from a passionate pastry chef who got mad after burning his pignolis."

"You lost me."

"On the day we met, I was wandering the streets of Naples. The most handsome man I'd ever seen stormed out of a bakery and almost knocked me over. His face was red, and even though I didn't understand a word he said, I knew he was angry. Any rational person would have walked away, but I had all this anger bottled up inside of me, and it exploded, and I yelled back at him. His entire demeanor changed, and he stopped yelling and wanted to make sure I was okay."

"That's quite a meet-cute," I said.

He smiled, the first smile I'd seen since he arrived at my house. "He wasn't yelling at me. He was yelling at his new oven. He couldn't get the temperature right, and he burned four batches of cookies in a row." He shook his head at the memory.

A breeze caught hold of my hem and tossed it around my legs. I rested back against the swing and looked up at the moon. It was a sliver moon, the thinnest slice glowing against an otherwise midnight sky. A cloud passed over it, hiding it briefly and then revealing it a moment later as the cloud continued on its way. The world turns. Life goes on. We can't always see what's right in front of us.

While we sat in silence, Jimmy's team flooded out of my garage. Several men climbed into trucks and drove off. JJ and Jimmy attacked the light fixtures. It appeared they were done with their work, but I didn't want to risk leaving Paulie —or allowing Paulie to leave me—by going over to check in with them, so I remained on the swing.

Paulie finally spoke again. "I went to Italy in search of a fresh start. I got Paolo. My whole life changed in one after-noon, but when he said he would move to the States to be with me, I was too scared to tell him the truth."

"A lie of omission is still a lie. It's going to come out. If you love him, if you believe he loves you, if you genuinely want to build a future with him, then you have to tell him. You just said Paolo was your fresh start. Don't you owe it to yourself to let him be part of your whole life, not just the part that started when the two of you met?"

Our conversation was interrupted by Jimmy's approach. "Hey, Madison," he called out. "I'm not interrupting anything, am I?" He got closer and kept his eyes on Paulie. I could tell he was curious about this man I sat with in the dark, but I felt no need to explain the unexpected visit.

"Not at all," I said casually. "How's the pool coming?"

"We're done." Jimmy twisted at the waist and looked over his shoulder at the garage. He pulled his baseball hat off and scratched his head and then put the hat back on and looked at me. "The concrete slabs will settle a bit overnight, but we leveled out the ground with sand and gravel first, so what you see now is what you'll see tomorrow. You wanna check it out?"

I peered past him. The lights were out, and the street was lit by the occasional streetlamp. "Tomorrow will be fine," I said.

Jimmy looked at Paulie again and then back at me. "You mentioned a bonus?"

"Oh, right." Caught up as I was in the conversation with Paulie, I'd completely forgotten the cash incentive. I stood up and smoothed out the folds of my dress. "Can you give us a moment? I'll meet you by the house."

Jimmy nodded.

I waited until Jimmy was out of earshot before I looked at Paulie. "You know how I feel about this," I said, "but it's up to you. I won't involve myself in your life any further."

Paulie stood up. He looked tortured by the events that were unfolding around him, and I wanted to believe, despite his past crime, that he was innocent of the current one. I reached forward and grasped his hand and squeezed. He squeezed back.

"I honestly wanted to help you," he said. "But if I had any idea you replaced Olivia on the commercial, I never would have offered. That woman was trouble."

"With all due respect, when she called the cops on you after you stole a car, she was reporting a crime."

Paulie's smile faltered. "Is that what you think? That she was doing her civic duty by calling the police?"

"That's what the articles I read said. Why? What did I miss?"

"I'm not proud of who I was after school. I got into some financial trouble and couldn't pay my bills. I couldn't get a decent job to save my life. I answered an ad to manage an up-and-coming starlet and found out it was Olivia. She needed a manager to help her transition from topless dancer to the mainstream media. She was professional and driven, and I needed the money so I accepted. Worst mistake of my life."

"Was she easy to work with?"

He shook his head. "If she had talent other than what I saw in that interview, she didn't use it. Olivia was convinced her sex appeal was her ticket. I tried to tell her the only way to break out of the stripper mold was to play against type, and that before she focused on the money, she had to focus on the work. Every time I suggested an audition to her, she turned down the roles because the money wasn't good enough. After a while, I started to suspect she was making money through illegal channels, but when I confronted her, she denied it."

"How long did you keep her on as a client?"

"Until I went to jail." He stared off into the distance. I knew there was more, but instead of prompting him to talk, I waited patiently for him to continue. "Olivia set me up. She said she bought a new car and needed me to move it for her. She told me where she kept her keys. I did what she asked and half a mile from where the car was parked, the cops pulled me over. She called it in as a theft and I was arrested."

"Why would she do that?"

"Olivia Jean was an opportunistic person who only thought of herself." He shook his head. "I don't know if she wanted a manager or if she wanted a scapegoat, but either way, it was best for her if I was out of the picture. I couldn't afford an attorney so I went with the public defender, and when the prosecution painted a picture of a gay man who'd been evicted from his last two apartments and couldn't pay his bills, the judge sentenced me to ten years."

"Didn't you appeal?"

"No. I was at rock bottom. It felt like where I belonged. I served my time and put the experience behind me. Olivia's been breaking the law with impunity for as long as I've known her, and it looks like someone decided her number was up."

TWENTY-SEVEN

I DIDN'T KNOW WHAT TO SAY. IN THE SPAN OF ONE conversation, Paulie had confessed to his role in a vehicular theft and how it had led to him finding the love of his life and then circled back around to the motive he'd have for killing Olivia. Between my visit with Paolo earlier and now this conversation, I'd gotten comfortable with him while chatting on my outdoor swing, but now, traces of the anger that I'd seen before put me on high alert.

I pointed to the house. "I have to attend to business. Captain Allen is due any minute, and frankly, it's been an exceedingly long day."

Paulie stepped toward me, and I put my hands up and stepped back. He stepped back too. His expression changed from sadness to hurt as he realized my actions were based in fear. "You still think I could have hurt her, don't you?"

"Go home and talk to Paolo," I encouraged. "Of everything you told me tonight, he—your life with him and the children—that's the most important."

I watched Paulie cross my yard and drive off. I remained by my swing for a moment longer. In one week, I'd gone from a thriving business owner to a marriage counselor. I'd taken two jobs: one for the police and one designing an ice cream parlor, and somehow those two things had converged and brought me into a big, fat mess.

This wasn't the first time I'd gotten involved in the personal matters of a client. There'd been Connie and Ned Duncan, clients who'd become friends who'd then gotten divorced. There was the husband-and-wife producer team who lived here temporarily and optioned the story of Hudson's life to be turned into an upcoming movie. There'd been the pajama factory an elderly friend I'd made during my morning swims had bequeathed to me when she died, which had led to me uncovering all kinds of secrets.

Did everyone have secrets? Was I lying to myself to think that I didn't?

I thought I lived my life out in the open, but the truth was, when I moved from Pennsylvania to Dallas, it was with an eye on the same fresh start Paulie had wanted when he went to Italy. If my past hadn't caught up with me, I would have pretended it didn't exist. Even now with Tex, we rarely talked about the people we were before we got together, though I was certain his closet held far more relationship skeletons than mine.

Yet...here I was having a pool installed in secret.

Tex understood my job and knew about my plans for expansion. He knew I often used my house to decorate and photograph for my portfolio, and he was my biggest cheer-leader when it came to taking risks. He'd seen me come out the other side of the lawsuit where I nearly lost everything and watched me get back onto my feet. He wanted me to succeed.

And I was acting as if his knowledge of the project would somehow diminish it. I was acting overly possessive about my business. As if him knowing what I was doing would make it less valuable. This was a trigger. A fear of trusting someone. I'd been operating as a solopreneur for so long that the idea of expansion made me vulnerable to criticism.

I vowed to stop getting personally involved with my clients. It never led anywhere good.

Jimmy was waiting for me by the front of my house. I unlocked the door and led him inside. He followed me tentatively, stopped in the solarium, and held up his hands. "I'm dirty from the job site," he said. "I can wait here."

"Nonsense. I'm a decorator. Demolition is my middle name." I walked farther into the house and pulled the envelope of cash that Billings had given me out of the walnut sideboard in my living room. I flipped open the envelope and pulled out a wad of cash then counted out five thousand. I put the remaining half back in the envelope and held the cash out toward Jimmy. "Thank you."

He took the envelope and held it up. "Thank *you*," he said back. "My wife's been angling for a new refrigerator." He tucked the envelope in his back pocket and cocked his head in the direction of the backyard. "That guy out there a friend of yours?"

"He's a client."

"He lives out there by Saint Frances Park, doesn't he?"

"I really shouldn't give away where my clients live."

"Ah, no problem," he said with a laugh. "I'm fairly sure we're neighbors. I helped him and his partner get this awful purple bathtub into their house. Didn't want to say anything, but whatever they paid for it was too much."

I stifled a smile. How was it possible for Jimmy to stand in the middle of my house, having walked through a sunshine-yellow kitchen into a living room with a display of atomic starburst clocks on one wall and a macrame owl on the other, and say such a thing?

"Nice guy, though. He helped my wife change a flat tire last week. He was out for his morning walk and just stopped to help her. It's nice to have neighbors like that."

"When was this?" I asked.

"Friday."

"What time?"

"Why?" he asked suspiciously.

I could hardly tell my pool contractor that the friendly neighbor who'd helped his wife with the flat tire was a person of interest in a murder investigation or explain why I was entertaining him at night, but if Paulie had been a good Samaritan at the same time Olivia had been killed, then he'd have an alibi.

"You know something about that guy you want to tell me?" he asked, this time more demanding.

"I'm doing a job at his house, and his partner suggested a secret installation."

"Like what we did here with your pool?"

"Something like that. Paulie—that's his name—works

erratic hours, so I'm having a tough time figuring out when I can get into and out of the house without him knowing. You said something about his morning walk, and I thought if he goes for a walk at the same time every morning, I could plan around that."

"Sure, okay. He passes our house around ten till eight every morning. The other day, that tire kept him there for forty minutes. He's like clockwork. But I can do you one better. You tell me when you want to get in, and I'll have my wife invite him over for coffee to say thank you." He chuckled. "She's a talker, that one. She'll keep him tied up indefinitely."

My heart soared. Paulie had an alibi. I couldn't wait to tell Tex!

I sent Jimmy on his way. It was just after ten, and I was exhausted. I hopped into the shower and changed into a pair of light-blue silk pajamas with frog closures. The rain had started during my shower, and a steady stream of rainfall pelted against my windows. I climbed into bed. Seconds later, Rocky hopped up onto the coverlet, and not long after that, I fell asleep.

THERE ARE reasons why Feng Shui experts tell you not to keep your phone by the bed, the most important of which is the effect an unexpected ring coming in the middle of the night has on your sleep. I woke, disoriented, and it took me a moment to shake loose the cobwebs and answer. To my surprise, it was only eleven thirty; I'd been asleep for less than two hours.

"Hello?" I croaked.

"I just got off work. Did I wake you?"

I closed my eyes and inhaled and exhaled. "Is this Captain Allen?"

"You're tired. Go back to sleep. I was going to come over, but I'll head to my place."

Another inhale. Another exhale. "No," I said. "It's fine." I closed my eyes and leaned back against the headboard. There was something I wanted to tell Tex, and it took a moment to remember. "Paulie has an alibi," I mumbled. "The pool guy told me."

"I thought you didn't swim this morning." Headlights flashed against my windows, and I heard a car out front.

"Mmmmmmm hmmmmm," I said. I sank back down under the covers.

"I'm here. Don't bother getting up. The rain is getting worse. I'm going to park in the garage, and I'll let myself in."

"Garage," I repeated. I was about to doze off with the phone receiver cradled to my chest when I realized what Tex had said. I sat straight up, instantly alert. "Garage!"

I jumped out of bed. Rocky was startled. I shoved my feet into my Jacques Levine slippers, and I raced downstairs and outside. There was no sign of Tex's Jeep.

It was dark. Jimmy had disconnected the interior lights to the garage when he started construction, and there'd been no point reconnecting them since the existing structure was going to be removed after the big reveal. As my eyes adjusted to the darkness, I crept closer to the garage. That was when I saw one of the bays was open.

I heard water. And cursing. Lots and lots of cursing. A small light flickered from inside the garage, and I rounded the corner and discovered a surprise bigger than the one I'd hoped to spring on Tex: a waterlogged police captain with a waterlogged Shi Chi puppy, both in my new pool, along with an equally waterlogged Jeep.

TWENTY-EIGHT

THE SOLE LIGHT IN THE GARAGE CAME FROM THE HEADLIGHTS to Tex's Jeep, now submerged in six-foot-deep water. The water closed over the roll bar. The addition of the car to the pool displaced a sizeable amount of water that now covered the concrete pavers Jimmy's team had just installed.

Tex swam to the side of the pool. Wojo doggy paddled next to him. Tex picked up Wojo and set him on the deck and then pulled himself out. He was still wearing the suit and tie he'd worn for his press conference, though it was now plastered to his muscular figure.

"Surprise," I said.

Wojo stood on the deck and shook his body, spraying water off in all directions. Tex walked toward me. The light from his car made the pool glow and created an unusual light source.

"When did you do this?"

"The contractor broke ground after you left for your latest recruiting trip. They've been coming to work while you're at the office."

"You told me you were having concrete poured."

"That was a lie," I confessed. He was two feet away from me, and from his expression, he was about as pleased that I'd lied to him as he was about having driven his car into the pool. "You've been stressed. More stressed than usual. You've done a lot to help me out, and on top of your regular responsibilities, you've been busy trying to change the perception of the police department."

His expression went from annoyance to surprise. I considered that a positive. "The police force is to you what Mad for Mod is to me. And until you regain the public's trust, it feels like you're going to lose your business. The commercials, I get it. I told you a long time ago that being a decorator and being a detective aren't that different."

"You think you know how I feel?" he asked.

"I *understand* how you feel. There's no way for me to know for sure."

"There's one way." And in one swift motion, he scooped me up and carried me to the side of the pool. I kicked and wriggled and did my best to get loose, but even I knew the struggle was pointless. Moments later, I knew exactly how Tex felt: cold and wet.

I'D LEFT a stack of vintage beach towels inside the garage, and we dried off and then ran to the house to get warm. Any anger that might have come from Tex driving his Jeep into the pool dissipated the moment he tossed me into the water. The fact that I emerged with blue silk pajamas plastered to my body didn't seem to hurt. Tex was predictable that way.

We took a joint shower with the drain stopper in the tub so warm water backed up around our ankles and used up the better portion of the hot water before we got out. Tex handed me a towel and then wrapped one around his hips and used another to rub his hair.

"I gotta hand it to you, Night. That's a big project to keep secret."

I wrapped a large bath sheet around my torso and used a second one to turban my blond hair. I took a fluffy terrycloth robe off the back of the door and pulled it on. "It helped that you were preoccupied."

"Homicides will do that."

"I meant the recruiting," I said. "You've been on three trips this month, all before Olivia's murder. My last day at the airplane hangar was the day the original film crew showed up to shoot your commercial."

He studied me carefully. "Original film crew," he repeated.

"Yes. Remember? My director was Denton Gold, who was your director too. When the Fraleighs saw my commercial, they decided to go with me instead of her. I assumed Denton would still be the director, but they replaced him with Jules."

"What's your take on her?"

"Jules?"

"The last time you mentioned her, you were cagy because of her connection to your ex-boyfriend. Now you've worked with her. You think she's qualified to film that commercial?"

"She's aloof," I said. "She doesn't mingle with the crew, and she doesn't joke around. Even when they're within earshot, she ignores them. It's like there's this barrier around her, and she doesn't want anyone to penetrate it."

"Could be she's nervous," he said. "Lot of eyeballs on this job."

"Or it could mean something else," I supplied.

Tex pulled on a police academy sweatshirt he left at my house and a pair of black jersey sweatpants. He sat on the corner of my bed and watched me root through an early-sixties walnut dresser for a fresh pair of pajamas. Despite the fifty-degree temperature and the long, hot shower, the dip in the pool had left me with a chill I couldn't shake. I stuck my hand under the bottom of the pile and pulled out pink flannel PJs printed with white daisies. I pulled the elastic-waist bottoms on first and then shed my robe and pulled on the top. It had a yoke trimmed in white lace and three little buttons down the front.

Tex studied me. "Flannel," he said. He looked down at his crotch and shook his head and then looked up at me. "I'm probably too tired anyway."

"You're incorrigible." I threw my terrycloth robe at him.

We moved from the bedroom down to the kitchen, where I turned on a space heater and put the remaining Entenmann's hot cross buns on the table. Tex grabbed one before I had a chance to sit.

"You got coffee?"

"It's almost one."

"I'm immune to caffeine."

I poured him a cup and a glass of juice for myself. "How'd it go tonight?"

"It didn't." He helped himself to a second bun. "Do you know what today is?" he asked.

"Monday?" I glanced at the clock. "Make that Tuesday."

Tex continued as if I hadn't said anything. "It's the Fraleighs' anniversary. Or it was. Edward cut our meeting short so he could get flowers for his wife before they went out to dinner."

"And?"

"And after dinner, he took her to see *The Barber of Seville* at the Dallas Opera."

"Why would he book the rough cut on the night of his anniversary?"

"He didn't."

I set down my glass. "To people like me, one thirty is the middle of the night. The only brain activity I'm expected to use is from an REM cycle."

Tex put a third bun on his plate but didn't pick it up. "Edward Fraleigh didn't set up a viewing of the rough cut of the commercial tonight. I checked with his office, and they knew nothing about that."

"Then where have you been for the night?"

"I staked out the address you gave me. Somebody told you to show up there, and I wanted to know who."

"Did anybody show?"

"Yes. Drew Billings." He spun his plate a quarter turn

and assessed the third bun from a different angle then sat back and rested his arms on the table. "So did Jules. I waited there for two hours, and they were the only ones to show. Either she's involved in this, or she's cheating on her fiancé."

TWENTY-NINE

"DREW BILLINGS WAS THE ONE TO HIRE ME," I SAID. "BUT when Effie tried to reach him, his mailbox was full. She called Commissioner Fraleigh's office, and they told her he'd been fired."

"That's right. Billings no longer works for the commissioner."

"You knew this. You've known this all along. Why didn't you tell me?"

He kept his eyes trained on me but didn't say anything. We'd taken a turn onto my least-favorite one-way street.

"Can you at least tell me why he was let go? It seems suspicious that everything happened the day he offered me the job. He showed up at the pool with an envelope of cash and directions to the furniture store. Within the hour, Olivia was dead, and I discovered her body."

"Billings worked for the commissioner's office in an

undefined role. Technically, he was a consultant on operations, policy, and due diligence."

"Did you like him?"

"Nobody liked him. We tolerated him. He had Fraleigh's ear on a number of cases and advised him on the future of the police departments in Dallas."

"Why did he get fired?"

Tex rubbed his forehead. "Nobody's talking about that. I called around to my counterparts at other divisions, and most are happy he's gone. The official statement from Fraleigh's office is that the expansion of the Dallas Police Departments required a reorganization from within, and all consulting contracts were terminated to free up money for salaried positions."

"Do you buy that?"

"If it's true, then it's possible Billings agreed to oversee the new commercial as the final part of his contract."

"And if it's not true?"

"That's the thing. Billings was in the inner circle. He knew an awful lot about police business, and he's just the kind of guy to use that knowledge to blow the lot of us to pieces."

DESPITE TEX'S cup of coffee and two and a half hot cross buns, we fell asleep shortly after going to bed. My internal alarm woke me at five thirty, the time I usually got up to go swim. Tex was fast asleep. We'd been on different schedules for weeks now, and I wasn't wired to function on less than six hours of sleep, so I rolled over and closed my eyes, careful not to wake Tex. He required less sleep than I did, but he was a year older than I was, and I refused to believe age had caught up with me first.

I dozed back asleep, and when I woke again, Tex was on his back, staring at the ceiling with his arms behind his head.

"You're awake," I said.

"Nightmare. I dreamt I drove my Jeep into a pool."

I propped myself up. "You did."

He closed his eyes. "The fun never stops with you, Night."

We got up and took turns in the bathroom. I dressed in a peach-and-white houndstooth tunic with a roll collar, a pair of matching stirrup pants, and white leather Keds. I took the dogs out for a walk around the block while Tex checked out the pool with the benefit of daylight. As I rounded the third corner of the block, I joined him.

We hadn't bothered closing the garage door bay after Tex's accident, and with the benefit of daylight, I saw the most ridiculous sight imaginable. Aside from a flawless installation, there was a large vehicle in the middle. It would take a team of experts to get it out. I wondered what Tex's insurance would say about something like this.

"Who did the work on this?" he asked.

"Jimmy's Pools of Dallas."

"They did a decent job." He stood alongside the pool with his arms crossed. "Didn't something like this happen in one of your Doris Day movies?" I nodded. "You weren't secretly hoping for this, were you?"

"I like to think I'm more evolved than that."

"But?"

"I'm not going to say it wasn't funny."

We let the dogs have the run of my house. I dropped Tex at the police station. He had a fleet of squad cars at his disposal and a cousin who ran an impound lot. I was no expert on cars in pools, but it seemed wise to get the Jeep out of mine sooner rather than later, so I called the company that had lifted the roof off my garage, explained the problem, and waited for them to arrive. I let Effie know I'd be at the satellite office, and while I waited for the work crew, I got to work myself.

The mood boards I had made for my consultation with the Mangieris were still sitting on my desk, and I fell in love with my concept all over again. It seemed like a lifetime ago that I sent that email thanking Paulie for his help and inquiring about when we could meet, but it had only been a few days. So much had happened since then, not just in my world but for both of them. They had a lot to discuss, and none of it involved ice cream.

But I'd been hired to do a job, and a job I planned to do. With my new concept in place, I double-checked my inventory of white floor tiles and, when I discovered broken tiles in every box, changed course. I researched the pros and cons of pouring a concrete floor vs using epoxy and ultimately chose epoxy for both durability and non-skid features.

By the time lunch rolled around, I had finished the design. From the suspended ball light fixture with a red glass globe to represent a cherry to frothy white curtains hung on *tromp l'oeil* windows depicting scenes of Italy to George

Nelson coconut chairs to a white epoxy floor speckled with tiny flecks of mint, pink, and dark, chocolatey brown that reciprocated the SparkleLam™ counters, it was cute, refined, and whimsical—my three favorite things.

I left my desk and rooted around the miscellaneous broken fixtures for inspiration. It came in the form of a vintage Bilt-Rite Baby Stroller from the fifties. Made of chocolate-brown vinyl, it had a tear in the hood, and two of the wheels were flat. I doubted it was safe for its intended purpose, but modified, it would make a wonderful gelato cart.

I took the cart out back, removed the torn and broken hood, and gave it a thorough cleaning. While it dried, I rooted through sets of plastic stencils for something that felt appropriate. At the bottom of the box was a set of dry transfer letters. I flipped the letters over and assembled the words "Mangieri Gelato," taped them together on the back, and then carried them outside and applied them to the side of the vintage stroller. I outfitted the inside of the stroller with an Igloo cooler and then pieced together pieces from the torn stroller hood to cover the lid. When it was complete, it was among the most charming accessories I'd ever created.

I left my desk and rooted through boxes of light fixtures until I uncovered three brass double-cone wall sconces. I set them by the door with the bundles of paper straws Effie had acquired for me at Trader's Village. So much of the design revolved around my ice cream–inspired color palette that settling on the bowls to use for serving had provided a challenge until I remembered a collection of melamine bowls I'd gotten from the estate of Neena Martin, a recently deceased great-grandmother who'd entertained her family until the tender age of ninety-five. With an extended family that numbered twenty-five before counting in-laws, she'd kept her cupboards full of unbreakable dishes for every occasion. I pulled together enough mismatched pieces from Boonton-ware in princess pink, Oneida avocado, and Dallas Texas-Ware in white to make a statement. I planned to stack them on the shelves next to transparent glass jars of chocolate chips, sprinkles, and almonds, which would carry the deep brown hue up to the walls.

After stacking my supplies for the ice cream parlor installation, I took a break and left my office to check on the car-removal process. A tow rig and two fire trucks were parked willy-nilly in the street by my garage. Jimmy's truck was there, and he and his son conversed with a team of men I hadn't yet met. I steeled myself for whatever they'd throw at me and approached them.

"If I knew you wanted a place to park your car, I might have suggested a different concept," Jimmy joked.

"I told you I wanted to surprise Captain Allen," I said. I pointed to the car and added, "He was definitely surprised."

Now that the pool was no longer a secret, there seemed no reason to leave the garage standing. I stood back and watched as a demolition team—apparently they were avail-able when urgent jobs like this guaranteed their income—secured cables to the roof of my garage and the tow rig lifted it and set it, in one piece, on a flatbed truck. The tow rig turned back to the pool, where a team of divers attached a giant chain to the Jeep and then climbed out of the pool. The tow rig driver lifted the waterlogged Jeep out of the pool and set it alongside my front hedges. I was impressed; it was a decent parallel park job.

As I watched the firefighters and tow rig crew tackle the job, I was reminded of the team that had worked on the commercial shoot. How they'd worked together to get their job done and how Jules had kept her distance from them the whole time. There was something off about her behavior. Tex had seen her with Billings last night, and we knew Billings had nothing to do with the commercial, so what was her angle?

Since I wasn't needed at the pool site, I returned to my office. I picked up my phone and found the text from one of the PAs and texted him back, asking if there was any word from Jules on the commercial rough cut?

Reply: *She's at her studio working on edits.*

It was, by all purposes, an invitation.

Jules was hiding something, but I didn't know how, if at all, it related to the case. And while I knew my relationship with Tex was on solid footing, I felt protective toward Hudson, a man from my past who didn't deserve a woman who played games. I wasn't sure what Jules was up to, but a good woman-to-woman talk might yield some answers.

THIRTY

REMOVING VEHICLES FROM POOLS WAS NOT MY AREA OF expertise, so I left the workers to finish the job unsupervised. I looked up the directions I'd been given to Jules's studio and headed out. Jules was hiding something, though I couldn't begin to imagine what.

I pulled into the parking lot of a large concrete building. A long blue banner ran the perimeter of the building, occasionally announcing businesses within. On the far end was a sign that said JULES OF DENIAL. A smaller sign, attached to the entrance, repeated the company name and was followed by Video Production Company. I parked next to Jules's Fiat and entered.

Inside the building was a concierge desk, and behind the desk was Jules herself. She was writing something and didn't look up. I cleared my throat to subtly get her attention, and when she did notice me, she blanched. She stood quickly and closed the notebook in front of her all in one motion.

"Madison," she said. Her hand flew to her ear, where she fingered her dangly earring nervously. "What are you doing here?" she asked.

"Hi, Jules. I'm sorry if I startled you." As I stood in front of her, I realized I hadn't thought much about what I planned to say when I arrived. And here I was, alone with her, a person whose name was on the suspect list in my small vintage handbag. It would have been among the dumber things I'd done if I had any real reason to suspect Jules, but aside from a few suspicious actions on her part, there was nothing to link her to Olivia except her presence at Fraleigh Furniture the day Olivia died.

"I—I wanted to talk to you," I said.

"Is this about the commercial?" Before I answered, she said, "I showed Mr. Billings the rough cut last night, and he said he was going to take it to Commissioner Fraleigh today. I was hoping to hear something soon. If we must reshoot, I might have to find a whole new crew."

I'd intended to approach Jules in a calm and friendly manner, but something about her answer struck a nerve. She'd been aloof from the first day I showed up on set, and with the mention of Billings, I knew she was covering up something.

Before I knew I was going to respond, I moved forward and put my hands on the counter. "I know you're lying," I said. "I came here to talk to you about Hudson. I thought that's why you've been cold toward me, and if we're going to work together, I thought we should clear the air. But now, I think I should call the police and tell them you're working with Billings. I don't know what you're up to, but I'm sure they'd like to ask you a thing or two."

Jules looked at me as if I'd lost my mind. "Of course, I'm working for Mr. Billings. So are you, by extension. He's our liaison to the police commissioner."

"No, he's not. Billings was fired before our commercial shoot started."

"That's not possible. I met with him last night. He said he was going to review the rough cut with Commissioner Fraleigh today."

I studied Jules's face. She looked as if she feared me more than I feared her. "Commissioner Fraleigh took his wife away for the weekend to celebrate their anniversary. They left yesterday afternoon. His office knew nothing of a rough-cut screening. But you met with Billings last night. Alone. Why?"

"How do you know that? Are you following me?"

I countered her question by repeating my own. "Why did you meet with Billings?"

"I already told you. He hired me to film the commercial. He paid me in cash. That's the only way I was able to pull together a skeleton crew so quickly. Why else would he do that?"

From the moment I'd entered this building, I'd been aware that Jules lacked the connection to Olivia that my other suspects had, and once again, I felt like I was talking to a person who wasn't aware of the events surrounding her. "Did you know Olivia Jean?"

"The woman whose body you found that first day of shooting?" she asked. "No. The police asked me about this too. Why does everybody keep asking me about her?" She stood up and stared at me. Her eyes were wide and red, and blotches of purple became visible on her neck and collarbone.

"You were the only other person present when I found her body," I said. "I found her because you directed me out back. You told me to go outside, and when I went outside, Olivia was dead in the parking lot. And the way you act, it's suspicious. You don't talk to anyone on the set. You pretend you can't hear people when they're five feet away from you."

"You don't understand what it's like to be in charge," she said. "Everybody has a question, everybody calls your name, everybody needs you. You don't understand what that's like."

"You're right. I work for myself. I don't have people calling my name all day, but when people talk to me, I respond." I hadn't expected hostility to creep into my voice, but it was there nonetheless. I'd told myself I wouldn't judge Jules because of her relationship with Hudson, but I couldn't help myself. He deserved a woman who would be there for him, not one who would ignore him, and if what I'd seen was any indication, Jules could tune out people as easily as if she were switching off a radio.

She reached up to fiddle with her earring again, except this time, it wasn't her earring she fiddled with. It was a tiny device that she removed from her ear. She stared at the piece of pinkish-beige plastic for a moment and then set it in her palm and held her palm out. "It's my hearing aid," she said. She kept her eyes averted. "I had a pair, but I lost one on the set."

Flashcard images of Jules at the store slid through my

memory. Every suspicious action could be explained by an inability to hear clearly. "You dropped something right before I tried to talk about the cue cards," I said. "You said it wasn't important."

"I don't want anyone to know," she said. "I don't want to be treated differently. I don't want people to think of me as not capable."

"Nobody would think you aren't capable."

"You don't know what the film industry is like." She tipped her head to the side and fit the tiny hearing aid back into her ear canal then mussed up her hair to cover her ears. "This was my first commercial. My first directing job. This was a foot in the door."

"Who hired you?" I asked. It was a bold question considering my own tenuous hiring circumstances, but she didn't have to know that.

"Mr. Billings contacted me. He said he was looking for a commercial director who could work on a tight deadline. I jumped at the chance, and I called in every favor I have to get a crew."

"Then you put the crew together? Everybody there was your choice?"

"Not everybody. I didn't know about your publicist or acting coaches."

I didn't tell her they'd been a surprise to me too. "What about the production assistants? Or Aliyah? Or Bruce?"

"All mine," she said. "Bruce brought in a few people I didn't know, but that's normal."

We'd been standing in a face-off by the front desk of Jules's production company, and my knee had had enough of it. The problem was, I wasn't yet ready to leave. If Jules wasn't part of the plot to murder Olivia, then she'd been a victim of circumstance. And if Drew Billings had targeted her, there had to be a reason.

"Is there a place we can sit?" I asked. "My knee—I'm not used to standing indefinitely."

"Sure," she said. She left the front desk and flipped the lock on the door then led me into a waiting room that had a sofa and a scattering of chairs. I sat in a blue tweed chair, and she sat on the sofa. I stretched my leg out in front of me and ran my hands over my knee. It had been long enough since I'd injured it that the swelling only returned in extreme conditions, but a bit of stimulation never hurt.

As I rubbed my knee, I struck the conversation back up. "Have you talked to Hudson about any of this?"

She shook her head.

"Why not?"

"He doesn't like cops," she said. "Understandably, if you ask me."

If Jules had worked on the movie about Hudson's life, then I assumed she knew the source material for that case. And that case hadn't treated Hudson well. "Would he get mad if he heard you were doing a commercial for the police?"

"He's not like that. He doesn't tell me what to do."

"But you didn't tell him."

"I didn't want to bring up past ghosts."

"Those same ghosts led to him meeting you."

She stared at the arm of the sofa while a tiny smile played at the corners of her mouth. They must have talked about that, about how something tragic and awful had led to something unexpected and good. It was how I felt about Tex, though God only knew it had taken me a long time to get here. And yet "here" was not just an emotional state but a circumstantial state as well, and until Olivia's murder was solved, Jules would be haunted by those circumstances herself. I didn't want to tell her that the longer she went without dealing with this, the more difficult it would be to forget it had happened.

Our conversation lapsed into silence, and I found myself unsure what to say next. It was Jules who broke the awkwardness. "Do you want to see it?" she asked.

"See what?"

"The rough cut. I gave Mr. Billings a copy, but I have the original here." For the first time since I'd spoken to her, she softened and seemed friendly. "I could use some feedback, and considering you're the star, you'll probably be gentle."

THIRTY-ONE

I FOLLOWED JULES TO THE SCREENING ROOM. SHE HAD THE commercial saved to a flash drive and plugged it into a projector. I was used to screening 35mm movies at the Mummy, the local retro cinema house where I used to volunteer, and I had to admit, plug-and-play lacked the pageantry of a three-reel production.

Within seconds, my image filled a twelve-foot screen at the end of the room. I was in the yellow dress from the first day of filming. Despite knowing how much equipment had been brought into the furniture store, how much makeup Aliyah had used on my face, how many lights and fixtures and cables and screens had been positioned around me, it looked perfectly natural. I introduced myself and said my lines. The camera cut to me in the orange dress, where I turned to the camera and continued. A third cut put me in the blue dress, and the end of the commercial had me in pink.

It was...not terrible. And that not terrible had nothing to do with me and everything to do with Jules.

She switched the lights back on and turned to me. "What do you think?"

I grasped for something to say that would compliment Jules's directorial abilities while not overstating my talent—or lack thereof. "It's better than I expected."

"You hate it," Jules said. Her face colored, and immediately, I recognized the misunderstanding.

"The production value is fantastic. It's me I'm criticizing, not you. The police would have been better off with a professional. I wish I'd had you behind the camera of *my* commercial."

"Your commercial? You just said you're not a professional."

"I'm not." I pulled out my phone and cued up my commercial on YouTube. "I filmed a low-rent commercial for my decorating business. It was supposed to air a couple of times, but another advertiser backed out of his spot, and the local TV station slotted me in."

"Was the commercial effective?"

"I'm booked solid for the next three months."

"Then I'd say your director did an outstanding job."

I handed my phone to her. She tapped the play button and watched. Thirty seconds later, she handed the phone back. "I see what you mean."

I was self-aware, but it wouldn't have killed her to pretend.

I dropped my phone into my stirrup pants pocket. "That's

how Billings talked me into taking the job. He said after I finished filming the commercial for the police, the crew would film another one for me. Something less amateurish."

"He didn't tell me anything about that."

It seemed odd that Billings had gone to such lengths to get both Jules and me to the furniture store. It was odd enough that it was downright suspicious. If he planned to do in Olivia, was it simply so he'd have a building full of scapegoats at the ready?

I was lost in my thoughts about Billings and didn't hear Jules repeating my name. It wasn't until she reached out and touched my arm that I realized she was talking to me.

"Sorry to have startled you," she said, "but I just had a thought. Have you ever seen those commercials that say an iPhone has the power of Hollywood in your pocket?"

"Yes."

"You were promised a commercial, right?" She stood up and pulled her phone out of her back jeans pocket and then pulled a key out of the front pocket. She held both in front of her. "I shot my senior thesis on a camera with fewer bells and whistles than this."

"But I look," I glanced down at my outfit. Peach-and-white houndstooth pattern on a funnel neck tunic and matching stirrup pants. To any other woman, it was ridiculous. "—exactly like me," I finished. I stood up too. "Let me make a phone call, and then I'm good to go."

My tense relationship with Jules had pivoted a hundred and eighty degrees since I'd walked into her studio, but that didn't mean I was going to follow her blindly into the night. I called the police station, hoping to catch Tex. Instead, I got his Girl Friday.

"Imogene? Isn't it a little late for you to be answering the phones?"

"I've got two chapters left on my novel, and Captain Allen said I could work here as long as I answered the phone lines. It's dead quiet, which is more than I can say for Starbucks."

"I don't suppose Captain Allen is still there, is he?"

"No, he went to the Fraleighs' house for dinner."

"I thought they went away for their anniversary?"

"Mrs. Fraleigh came down with a cold, and they postponed. The commissioner didn't want to leave her alone tonight, so he asked Tex over so they could review the budgets. That's sweet, isn't it?"

"Don't you think it would be sweeter if he postponed business for one evening?"

"Cops are cops, Madison. They're married to the force."

I'd spent enough time with Tex to know she wasn't wrong. "You don't happen to have the Fraleighs' phone number handy, do you?"

"Sure, right here." She read off the number, and I glanced around for a pen, and then when I didn't see one, repeated it three times to commit it to my short-term memory. I thanked her, wished her luck on her final two chapters, and hung up.

I immediately typed in the memorized number. Arlene Fraleigh answered on the third ring. "Arlene? This is Madison Night."

"Oh, Madison! How delightful to hear from you. I keep

thinking about that powder room off the foyer. I don't think periwinkle is the correct shade after all. Maybe you could come over and help me sort through more swatches."

"Sure," I said. "When you're feeling better, give me a call, and I'll clear my schedule."

"Oh, honey, it's just the sniffles. Edward is too protective of me. I told him I'd be fine, but he wouldn't hear of us going away while I'm not a hundred percent."

"Yes, that's what I heard. You're lucky to have such a devoted husband. Speaking of which, I understand he's squirreled Captain Allen away for the evening?"

"Oh, yes, those two. Always planning something. Did you need me to find him for you?"

"That would be great, thank you." I held the phone to my ear and waited for her to return. Behind me, Jules had pulled on a man's blazer with sleeves that hung past her fingertips. She pushed the sleeves up to her elbows and draped her cross-body handbag over her shoulder. She was the picture of contemporary cool. I could see her with Hudson even though I'd never seen them together.

I held up my index finger and she smiled and pointed to the front doors. She held up a pack of cigarettes and a lighter, and I nodded.

Tex came to the phone. "It's me," I said. "I'm with Jules Staton at her production studio. She had no idea Billings wasn't on Fraleigh's payroll, and frankly, I believe her. She did the job she was hired to do, as much for the credit on her resume as for the money."

"I thought you said she acted suspiciously on set. Nasty backed that up."

"She wears a hearing aid. She dropped one and had to finish the commercial shoot without being able to hear out of one ear. It explains a lot."

"It does." His voice was muffled for a moment, and then he came back. "Are you heading home?"

"Soon," I said. "Give me a call when you finish whatever you're working on. I might be awake."

"I'm counting on it. Hold on, Arlene wants to talk to you again."

A moment later, the commissioner's wife returned to the phone. "Madison? Oh, good, you're still there. I was thinking yellow might make a nice statement. Maybe yellow and pink? But it is the guest powder room, and that might be a bit too feminine. What do you think?"

"I think I'll bring over my big book of bathrooms, and we can try to find inspiration in there."

"You know, if you're not afraid of a little bug, you could bring it over tonight. I'm sure Edward would like to know I had company while he was in his office with Captain Allen."

"Actually, I wanted to ask if it would be okay for me to shoot a late-night commercial at your furniture store? It's a spontaneous idea, but if you don't mind—"

"Of course!" she exclaimed. "I envy you, Madison, living the spontaneous life. Yes, by all means, film your commercial. I can't wait to see it."

I thanked her and hung up, feeling more at ease with the idea. I left Jules's studio and found her leaning against the Fiat.

I held up my phone. "I called Arlene Fraleigh to let her

know what we had in mind," I said. "She gave us her blessing."

"Perfect. I'll meet you there." She put out her cigarette and got into her car. I climbed into mine and followed her out of the lot.

It was after seven, and the sun was on the descent. In an hour, it would be dark. I was comforted by the fact that I'd talked to Tex, but there was still the awareness that I was returning to the scene of an unsolved crime. I could tell myself it was to film my commercial all I wanted, but deep down, I knew there was more to it. I felt like I'd—we'd—all missed something. And that didn't sit well with me.

On the way, I called Nasty. "What's up?" she answered.

"I'm on my way to Fraleigh Furniture to film a commercial with Jules Staton. Your surveillance cameras are still working, right?"

"They're on, but nobody's watching the feed. You plan to be there long?"

"No. We should be in and out in under an hour."

"I'll call one of the guys and tell him to keep an eye on you."

"Thanks."

I hung up and pulled into the furniture store parking lot. Jules had parked to the right of the entrance. I eased into the space next to her car and followed her to the door. She had it open quickly, and before you could say "abandoned furniture store," we were inside.

I dumped my handbag on a plastic-covered chair and followed Jules to the back, where we'd spent our time filming. She located the control box and threw a switch that bathed us in light.

"What do you have in mind?" she asked.

"You saw my first commercial. I stood in front of my camera, introduced myself, and told people what I do. I used free video editing software to add my website to the bottom of the screen."

"I think we can do better than that."

"That's what I'm hoping."

"Let's do a rough take so I can check angles. Say whatever you want, but you might want to make it sound good. If I get audio from one take and video from another, I can always piece it together."

"Okay."

"Five, four, three," she said, then held up her fingers in a peace sign and then her index finger and pointed at me.

"Hello, I'm Madison Night. I'm an interior decorator. You might have heard about me from my other commercial." I crossed my eyes and rolled them up. "Whew! That was a stinker! But you watched it, didn't you?" I waggled my finger at the camera. "And that's why I'm here. Because I wanted to visit you in your living room again and say—" I had an idea. I pointed to the corner of the room beyond Jules. "Is that your favorite lamp? That one you've got sitting in the corner with cobwebs on it. Shame on you. That's no way to treat the furniture." I moved around behind a chair and ran my hands lovingly across the top. "Furniture is meant to be loved. You interact with it every day, don't you?" I patted the chair and smiled at it. "Maybe if you pay more attention to your surroundings, they'll pay more attention to you." I realized what I'd just said made no sense and, after a moment of panic that I sounded like a fool, I glanced over both shoulders to see if I was being watched and then turned back to the camera. "I know and you know that that made no sense." I held my hand up on one side of my face and lowered my voice. "Just don't tell the sofa." I winked.

"Cut!" Jules said. She lowered her phone. "That was great. Why didn't you do that on set?"

"Because I was too worried about flubbing my lines in front of the crew."

"Forget your lines. Let's go again. Five, four, three..."

But this time, Jules didn't use the peace sign or her index finger or point to me to indicate it was time to talk. Her eyes widened, and her mouth gaped open.

"What's wrong?" I whispered.

"We're not alone," she whispered back. "There's someone behind you."

THIRTY-TWO

"TURN THE CAMERA ON AND FILM ME AGAIN. PRETEND YOU'RE checking the frame or the light. Try to get whoever it is on camera. I'll pretend you're filming me." Jules nodded. She held the camera aimed at me. "You've got to count me down like this is for real."

"Oh. Okay. Five, four, three," peace sign, index finger, point.

"Hi, I'm Madison Night, and I'm a local decorator. But you knew that, didn't you?"

It was at precisely that moment that the commercial was interrupted by a crash.

I turned and looked in the direction of the noise. One of the two large light fixtures that Bruce had maneuvered around our set was tipped, and a woman was pinned underneath. It didn't take long for her to cry out and identify herself.

"Oh, drat. I'm stuck. Madison? Yoo-hoo! Can you help me, dear?" All of which was followed by a sneeze.

It was Arlene Fraleigh. And curiously, she seemed to be in the same spirits she'd been in when I'd called her to ask for permission.

"Arlene?" I cried out. I turned to Jules and whispered, "Call 911. Tell them to send a car out here. Tell them it's an emergency." I didn't yet know the actual state of our emergency, but it seemed prudent to act now and think later.

Jules nodded and went in the opposite direction of me.

"I'm coming!" I added in an equally loud voice.

I stepped around the chairs and went behind me, locating Arlene on the floor under the 300D Mark II light. More accurately, her fur coat was under the light. She sat beside it. She didn't appear to be hurt but only annoyed. I rolled the light off the hem of her coat and then held out a hand to pull her up. She rose to her feet and swatted at her coat with brown leather gloves that she held in one hand. "Bugger," she said. "It's brand new," she said. "Edward, the dear. Never forgets an anniversary!"

I guided Arlene away from the light fixture to a row of chairs and indicated she sit. I sat next to her. "Arlene, what are you doing here? I thought you were home with a cold."

"Pish posh. I sneezed three times, and my husband canceled our anniversary trip. Everyone knows three sneezes indicates an allergy. It's one sneeze you have to worry about." She shook her gloves in my face while making her point.

"Does your husband know you're here?" I asked.

"No, but that can be our little secret!" she said. She

smiled broadly. She unclasped her handbag and pulled out a small silver flask and offered it to me.

Oh, no. Arlene had been tipsy at her party, and that had been the impetus for her dissatisfaction with Olivia as the commercial star. Was I reading this situation correctly? Had she snuck out to have some fun, or had she murdered a woman behind her father's abandoned furniture store and come here tonight to clean up a few loose ends?

Motive. Motive. Motive. The word hammered in my head. There'd been nothing about Arlene that connected her to Olivia other than her displeasure at having the exotic dancer become the face of the police testimonial. But even that had felt more loving wife with a request of her husband than angry spouse with hate-fueled demands.

"You girls keep going. I'm just going to sit here and watch. You won't even know I'm here. It's fascinating, you know. The cinema." She leaned forward and put her hands on mine. "You're so lucky, Madison!"

I wasn't sure what to say. Here were me and Jules in an abandoned building owned by Arlene. I was the reason she knew we were here because I'd called to get her permission. If anyone were to look suspicious out of the three of us, it wouldn't be her.

I turned my hands upside down and gripped Arlene's hands back. "Did you really come here to watch us film our commercial?"

"It's so boring at the house. Those two men, always meeting to talk about the police force. I knew when I married Edward that this was the life I signed up for, but you never really know, do you? You never really know that he can't let you into his job. It's not like being the wife of a businessman. There's always a barrier between us and them, Madison. They call it our safety, and at first, that seems charming. But we're not damsels in distress, are we? No, we are *not*." She took another swig from her flask.

This wasn't about Olivia's murder; it was about being cast aside on her anniversary. Replaced by Tex. Here was a woman who wanted fun in her life. She'd been fascinated by my life when we talked at her party, and that hadn't changed. The reason she kept inviting me and Tex around was to show her husband a positive influence.

Little did she know I was emotionally unavailable, and Tex was a recovering bachelor!

I didn't know where Jules had disappeared to, but as long as Arlene was there, I doubted we'd get anything done. I stood up and held my hand out to Arlene. "How about we get you home? I'll collect that pesky police captain who keeps showing up at your house, and you and your husband can have a proper anniversary."

She took my hand, and I pulled her to her feet. "I suppose you're right. You can tell your director he can stop hiding." She turned toward the back of the store and called out, "I know you're here. I saw you when I came in the back door. Come out, come out, wherever you are!"

The answer hit me as soon as that one little word, two letters long, came out of Arlene's mouth.

He.

Arlene didn't know Denton had been replaced on the commercial shoot, but she would recognize him. And she said she saw the director when she came in. That meant he was here.

Denton. The director who knew Olivia when she came to the set.

Denton, who closed his set for Olivia's commercial.

Denton, who'd been replaced by Jules and shouldn't have known the job continued at an alternate location.

I practically pulled Arlene toward the front of the store. I didn't know where Jules had gone. I pushed on the door to let us out, and the doors pushed back. They were locked.

We were trapped.

"There's no rush, Madison. We can go out the back."

"No, Arlene. We can't. Denton is back there."

"Actually, I'm not," Denton said. He pulled away from the shadows and walked toward us, revealing not only his twisted grimace but also the gun in his hand.

THIRTY-THREE

INSTINCTIVELY, I STOOD BETWEEN ARLENE AND DENTON. "Why are you here?" I asked him.

"Come on, Madison. Don't play games with me. We both know I can't let you leave."

Arlene put her hands on my shoulders and held me like a shield. "What's he talking about?" she asked. "Is this part of your commercial? Are you rehearsing?"

I turned my head to the side. "No, Arlene, I'm afraid not."

"Well, this is just foolish," she said. She let go of me, and I heard her rooting through her handbag. Seconds later, her arm extended past my right shoulder, her hand gripping a small black pistol. "You've got a gun, and we've got a gun. Do you see what I mean, Denton? This is foolish."

I stepped away from Arlene and considered letting her stand between me and the other gun-toting person in the store. I was woefully unprepared for a gunfight. Denton moved his aim from me to her and back to me.

I did not feel lucky.

"Why, Denton?" I asked. "Why did you kill Olivia?"

"You killed Olivia?" Arlene asked. "I can't wait to tell Edward I solved his case."

Denton looked disgusted, but that didn't change the angle of his gun. "Olivia was a scam artist. A grifter."

"What did she steal from you?"

"We were partners." He spat on the floor beside him. "She was good, too. Always had a plan. Ask the acting coach."

"Virginia? Did Olivia steal from Jumbos?"

Denton looked confused for a moment. "The other one. Paulie Mangieri. He never saw our swindle coming. She set him up to steal her car, and when he went to jail, she collected the insurance money. Thirty grand overnight. It pays to know an agent who will write out a fat check."

"You were the insurance agent," I reasoned. "That's what you did before you got into directing?"

"Before, during, what's the diff? It takes money to fund a movie. I'm four hundred thousand dollars in debt. Olivia was going to help me get out. This job was going to get her in with the police commissioner, and once we had that Rolodex, Olivia was going to shake down the city."

Arlene's gun fired. The unexpected sound ricocheted off the barren metal walls and reverberated. She said something to Denton, but the gunfire had temporarily deafened me, and while I could see her lips move, I couldn't hear what came out. She advanced toward Denton with her gun aimed at his chest. I didn't know where this was going, but it wasn't headed anywhere good. How was I going to explain the police commissioner's wife shooting a murderer before we had a confession?

Whatever Arlene said had changed Denton's demeanor. He backed away from her and held his hands up in the air. He still held the gun, but at least it wasn't pointed at me.

Arlene turned back to me, and her lips moved. I shook my head and pointed to my ears. She waved the gun toward a pile of rope sitting on the floor and then at Denton. He seemed to put two and two together about as quickly as I did and took off toward the rear of the store.

I couldn't let him leave. I ran up the aisle between the plastic-covered chairs, over the spot where I'd filmed all my commercials, and burst out the back door. Denton's body lay on the gravel. And Jules, sweet Jules, stood cowering behind the back door, covered with a dusting of sand that had leaked out of the torn sandbag she'd used as a weapon.

It wasn't a coffee urn, but it had done the job of detaining our killer while we waited for the police.

———

THE GREATEST HITS of Olivia and Denton filled the news for the next several days. Despite trying to keep the details quiet, the press got wind of how Arlene, Jules, and I had coerced a confession from the man who, along with Olivia, had been committing insurance fraud for decades. In his official confession, Denton called it a victimless crime. I thought about Paulie Mangieri, who'd spent ten years of his life behind bars for a theft Olivia had orchestrated. There were no victimless crimes. Someone always paid.

After the first wave of stories about Denton's murder of Olivia came the details about how he'd held Jules, Arlene, and me at the furniture store. The additional press did what I'd wanted all along: it boosted the visibility of Mad for Mod and attracted new clients.

Jules was linked to the upcoming movie about the pillow stalkings, which I suspected would help the box office returns in our neighborhood. If she played her cards right, she'd be directing movies and commercials in no time.

Of the three of us, it was Arlene Fraleigh who stuck the landing the best. She agreed to a press conference in which she detailed what had happened and sang the praises of the police, even though they hadn't been notified until after Denton was tied up with rope. It didn't surprise me to learn the police had a third round of commercials scheduled with her as the star. The last I'd heard, she was prepping to film her testimonial from her bed with her loving husband, the police commissioner himself, by her side. It was the ultimate anniversary present from and to each of them. You couldn't script a feel-good spot like that.

It was inevitable that the news dug up Paulie Mangieri's criminal past and how he'd served time for an auto theft orchestrated by Olivia and Denton. He'd already served his time, but public opinion cast him in a positive light. Tex saw an opportunity to book Paulie to speak to local high schools about his experience. It was the second positive thing to come into his life from an awful memory, and I couldn't help recognizing that sometimes, the worst moments of our lives are the ones that launch us toward the possibilities of our future.

Aliyah didn't come out of the fracas unscathed. As it turned out, she *had* been the one to break Olivia's fingernail, though quite by accident. When Olivia had turned up dead, Aliyah knew that fingernail could be used as evidence against her, and she took it home, where she hid it in plain sight among her nail supplies.

And the donuts? The odd clue that was never quite a clue was exactly what it seemed: distraction. Denton explained that in his statement as well. The morning of the murder, he snuck into the furniture warehouse and stole the fur-trimmed jacket from my garment bag to use as a disguise. After killing Olivia, he took the donuts to tamper with the crime scene and create confusion between Jules's and my statements. When he heard me on the other side of the door, fled. He wrapped the donut box in my jacket, destroying them with a jug of motor oil he had in his car, and ditching the bundle in a nearby dumpster. He thought the fabricated clue would give him the time necessary for him to find the money Olivia owed him and then get out of town.

But there was no money. Despite living the high life, entertaining at private parties around town, and positioning herself as a burgeoning actor with a burlesque background, Olivia was destitute. Her money had been bled off into self-aggrandizement to make her seem more important than she was. It was ironic that her murder gave her more publicity than anything she'd orchestrated in life.

As for me, not only did I get additional exposure from the attention of the news but a feature in a local magazine and an invitation to teach Intro to Decorating as a free course for my local paint store.

After putting the finishing touches on the Mangieris' ice cream parlor, having the pool drained and refilled, and approving a new round of commercials edited together from the footage Jules had shot for the police and the voiceover I'd improvised the night of the showdown, I finally discovered Tex's secret: on one of his recent recruiting trips, he'd bought a luxury sportfish model cruiser. And while I'd been busy hiding evidence of the new pool in the garage, he'd kept his new equipment locked away in the basement.

It wasn't until he drove his Jeep into my new pool that he recognized I'd been keeping secrets too, and the only reason we hadn't stumbled upon evidence of each other's was because we were too focused on keeping the ones we kept. To come clean, he invited me along on his trip to pick it up. And so this time, when I arrived at Dallas Love Field airport, it wasn't to film a commercial in an airplane hangar but to see a man about a boat.

Life with Tex might not have been glamorous, but it sure was interesting.

WANT MORE MADISON? Preorder *Love Me or Grieve Me*, Madison Night Mystery #10, coming October 2022!

ABOUT THE AUTHOR

National bestselling author Diane Vallere writes smart, funny, and fashionable character-based mysteries. After two decades working for a top luxury retailer, she traded fashion accessories for accessories to murder. A past president of Sisters in Crime, Diane started her own detective agency at age ten and has maintained a passion for shoes, clues, and clothes ever since. Find out more at dianevallere.com.

ACKNOWLEDGMENTS

Thank you to everyone who reads the Madison Night Mysteries! Your love of this character helps inspire me to keep dreaming up new mysteries for her to solve. It's a thrill to discover what she's up to every time I write one of her books, and I hope it's as much of a thrill for you to discover it on your end.

Special thanks to readers of the Weekly DiVa Club, especially those who volunteered to be dead people! We mystery readers are a little twisted. Special acknowledgments for this book go out to Gloria Jean Minnick, Robyn Konopka, Mark Baker, Lisa Benton, and Neena Martin. I hope you saw a bit of yourself in these pages. If you read the last line of the book—or rather, the line *after* the last line—then you know I'll be looking for more volunteers sooner than you know it.

Thanks to the team at Red Adept Editing, Henery Press, and my author friends who helped me brainstorm along the way. And a gargantuan thank you goes to Amy Ross Jolly for being my first reader.

Xo! —Diane

Want a bonus ebook that you can't get anywhere else? Join the Weekly DiVa Club and receive BONBONS FOR YOUR BRAIN, a collection of humorous essays about everything from writing mysteries to buying shoes to being the best version of yourself. Get the offer at dianevallere.com/weekly-diva.

ALSO BY

Lover Come Hack

Apprehend Me No Flowers

Teacher's Threat

The Kill of It All

Love Me or Grieve Me

Sylvia Stryker Outer Space Mysteries

Fly Me To The Moon

I'm Your Venus

Saturn Night Fever

Spiders from Mars

Material Witness Mysteries

Suede to Rest

Crushed Velvet

Silk Stalkings

Costume Shop Mystery Series

A Disguise to Die For

Masking for Trouble

Dressed to Confess

AUTHOR'S NOTE

Like any Madison Night book, *The Kill of It All* required research into things I never expected to learn. From how to install a fiberglass pool, to fishing boats, to Mary Kay sales director uniforms, to a whole host of decorating sites for installing an in-house ice cream parlor—the fun never stops in Madison's world!

Sign up to see an exclusive behind-the-scenes resource list for this book at dianevallere.com/thekillofitall-resources.